Penned State

BESTSELLING AUTHOR
S.I. HAYES

This book is a work of fiction. Any similarities to any person, place, or theory are in no way intended or to be inferred as fact or reference. The work is the particular property of the Author. Produced by human intellect and was in no way created or manipulated by an AI (Artificial Intelligence) program. It may not be reproduced in whole or in part or resourced by any entity, now or in the future, in any format without written permission by the author unless part of a Review, Interview, or Public push of the work and certain other noncommercial uses permitted by copyright law.
Contains adult situations. 17+ only
All Manuscripts and Designs By Human Designers With Licensed Images by Haney Hayes Promotions

CHAPTER 1

CALVIN

"Good morning Calvin!"

"Morning, Missus Singer!" I holler as I ride by on my metallic grey Beaumont seven-speed with a green racing stripe. I love my bike, it's lightweight, fun to ride, and not to mention great exercise. My mother, of course, would prefer I drove to school, but alas, I failed my driving exam, and with my class load this year haven't had time to reschedule. With all honesty, I just haven't even tried. Like I said, I like my bike.

I live in a sleepy little town in Delaware, called Cradle Bay, just south of New Castle. It's pretty, quiet, and mostly normal. Crime is low, at least in my surrounding neighborhood, and the school is good. Not that I have anything to really compare it to, but when I blew through the physical science and calculus books by Sophomore year, the teachers got together and with some online aid, managed to build me a more challenging curriculum.

When I start college, I'll already have enough credits for an Associates in

Information Sciences and Technology. Basically IT. You know Geek Squad type stuff. It's not my dream job, but it will be something that will help me get my foot in the door places. I mean everywhere needs IT guys these days. *Right?*

Maybe I'll go into criminal justice with a specialization on Cybercrimes? Eh, I got time yet. Not really. It's January, of my senior year, and we've just come back from our winter break. Yeah, it's a bit cold for the bike, but so long as temps stay above freezing-

"Cal!"

I turn my head, hearing a car horn honk. I smile as the beat-up 96' Ford Aerostar stops. The curly-haired head of my best friend Kaycee followed by the top half of her lurches out the window. "It's thirty-five degrees! You're gonna get pneumonia!"

"I'm fine!" I say, adjusting my helmet and pushing my glasses up. I watch in amusement as all five feet three inches of her leaps out of the van.

"Get off the bike, Cal. Get in the van, or I'm gonna break your spokes!" She pulls a pair of pliers out of her ass pocket.

"Hey, now not the spokes!" I grab her wrist. She stares at me with her freckled face and bird blue eyes.

"Do I have to repeat myself?"

"FINE!" I whine. "But, I wanted to stop at Dunkin' for a sandwich and a Great one."

"I swear the breakfast at school is *so* much better, but you go for that processed crap."

"I like the spicy turkey sausage." I get my

bike in the back of the van and hop in. I do have to say the van is old and smells like cigars and whiskey, but it is *warm*.

CHAPTER 2

KAYCEE

Calvin Archer Pennington the Fourth. Or, as I call him Cal, he has been my best friend since we were four. Our parents went to Cradle Bay High together, and our mom's at one point were even friends. Then his mom met Mister Pennington, and her nose got out of joint, and her head went clean up her ass. At least that's to hear my mother tell it. I'm inclined to believe it, seeing as I'm not even allowed in his driveway if either of them is home.

See, I'm from a broken and mostly poor family. We live in a not so great part of town. Same school district, cause it's all one district round here, but there is definitely a *class* divide. Thing is, Cal never much has been one to notice it. He accepts me, so the others do too. *Mostly*. There are a few guys. You know the ones that make the slumming it jokes? They get shut down quick though; I don't take any shit and besides, Cal and me? We ain't like that. Never have been. He's like a brother to me, I mean we've taken showers together, and that's since puberty. Hey, shit happens, and when you fall into the marsh, you wanna get that sludge off quick.

It's not that he's *unattractive*, by no means, any girl will be lucky to have him on her arm. He's tall, got blonde hair that curls up behind his ears, and greenish-blue eyes hiding behind those horn-rimmed glasses.

The problem is he's just so- goal orientated. It's not his fault, though. His parents really push. They want so much for him to be a doctor or a lawyer. He doesn't. Though in the long run, I'm sure he'll wind up going pre-law and transfer to like Stamford or Harvard after he does the basics. He's applied to a few Ivy Leagues to appease the 'rents, but I know he's got his heart set on UPenn. He had a favorite uncle that went, and my Grandfather is an alumnus as well, so he's heard about the school a lot.

We get to school, and I head off to my basic human classes while he goes to the Superman classes. We won't see each other again until lunch and then we have a free class. I have auto shop now and am glad for it; the Aerostar needs a tune-up.

"Hey! McLane? Earth to the *girl*? You done daydreaming about prom over there?"

My head turns on a swivel to the sound of Mister Joplin, chiding me.

"That's really a sexist thing to say, how do you know I wasn't going on in my head 'bout the ignition timing on this piece of work I brought in? I mean, it does need all the bells and whistles done. *Sir.*" I finish with disdain dripping from my lips. "Just because I'm a chick doesn't mean I don't have a bigger dick than most of this class."

"Alright, McLane, enough! Outside! Go see Koopersmith."

"Whatever, just don't fuck up my family car." I strip off the greasy overalls to hoot and hollers as I'm now in just booty shorts and a tank. What? It's hot under them overalls in the workshop!

"PUT SOME CLOTHES ON!" Mister Joplin demands as I grab my bag and skip out of the room like Polly Anna.

In the hallway, I kick off my sneakers to shimmy into a pair of jeans. I'm stumbling to get my feet back into the sneaks when I see Heath Cramer. He's like the only guy on the baseball team I like. We fool around from time to time, and by fool around, I mean fuck like rabbits in the old stairwell or the adjacent abandoned locker room. Girls gotta get her jollies someplace, and why not with a hunky dark haired blue eyed baseball God?

"Heya McLane. Pissin' Joplin off again?"

"You know it." I huff, grabbing his shoulder to steady myself. He takes the opp to cop a feel. I smack his hand. "Hey- *no*." I quip.

"No?" He retorts with a questioning attitude. "Since when?"

"I'm raggin'."

"Ahh, Gotcha. How 'bout a hummer then?"

"As if that did anything for me?"

"Me getting' off should complete you." Heath snickers.

"Get lost." I kiss him just wet and sloppily enough that he pops a boner. I give him a good squeeze. "Hmm..." I gruff. "Friday. After seven. Meet me at the back of Dunkin' I'll have the van."

"Keep rubbing." He moans happily.

"Nah." I shove him away and hoisting my bag head for the café.

CHAPTER 3

CALVIN

"You have a visitor, Mister Pennington."

I look at the door to my advanced physics class and see Kaycee waving me to her. "I'm sorry, Miss Warner. She just-"

"It's fine; you were just rechecking to pass the time anyhow. Go, but let's not make it a habit- *Miss McLane!*"

"No, Miss Warner!" Kaycee hollers then covers her mouth as she's shushed. The physics rooms are across from the library. "Sorry." She whisper-shouts to Missus Kinkel, the aging librarian.

"What's up, Kayce?" I ask stuffing my books into my bag while she stands next to me, shuffling from one foot to the other.

"I- it's just." She looks at the floor. "I thought I had credits. Mom said she loaded my card." She barely speaks, but I hear her.

"C'mon, I got you." I say, putting an arm around her. It's no wonder people think we're together most days. Lord knows I'd kill for her. Not that my parents like that idea much. Mother is convinced she's going to somehow ruin me. How could a sweet, caring, resourceful, not to mention a beautiful girl ruin me?

We get to the café, and the selection is not exactly *appetizing*. I mean, I can get a burger way better at *Applebee's*, or *Fuddruckers* in New Castle.

I look at her. "You wanna skip, don't you?" I ask as she bites her purple lip, pulling it into her mouth.

"They just finished the van." Her voice goes up in that adorable little squeak I just can't say no to.

"Where to?"

She squeals, grabbing my arm as she drags me back through to the hall. "*Kathy's.*"

"You wanna skip the day?"

"*Pul-ee-ase?*" She begs. "I'll love you forever."

I sigh, and she knows she's got her way. We grab the van, and it's one flash of the itty bitty titty committee to the security guard to make our escape.

"I really can't believe you let him take a pic this time." I scold her as we turn off toward Delaware City. It's closer than New Castle, and *Kathy's Crab Shack* has as you may have guessed it. The best crabs around.

"It's not like he can prove it's me. My face is covered. Besides, what's a little fodder in the spank bank for the poor guy?"

"You're a hero."

"Damn straight, I am. I should get a medal doing' all these good deeds."

"Oh, what other deeds you been doing that are so exceptional?"

"Getting you a life."

I look at her as she smirks. I hate that look. It means she's been scheming.

"What are you up too?"

"You'll see." She sing songs.

Ten minutes later, we're pulling up to *Kathy's*. It's a cool building with a space that looks like an actual lighthouse. It's also handicap accessible, which is why Kayce likes the place. She comes here with her Grandpa a lot. He's in a wheelchair; diabetes took his left leg. He's too big of a man for the crutches, and they are still working toward a prosthetic.

As we park, I see a girl leaning against the railing. She's got on a puffy jacket, covering what I'm assuming is a skirt, her black hair is swept up in a pony. Christ, she's even got on knee socks. If there's a sweater set underneath, I may die. I clear my throat.

"You see somethin' you like?" Kayce teases as the girl straightens up.

"What are you doing?" I say out the side of my mouth.

"Shut up; I'm tryin' to get you laid." My eyes bug as we step up the ramp.

"Hey, Kaycee." This girl has a soft sweet little voice on her.

"Jocelyn Pierre, meet Calvin Pennington the fourth." Kayce says all formal like.

I put out my hand to meet hers. "Cal, please."

"Okay, *Cal*. I'm starving; let's get inside. I already got us a table, if that's okay?"

"That works."

We follow her inside, and she shrugs off the jacket.

Fucking sweater set.
***

Turns out Jocelyn went to Cradle Bay too, just two years ahead of us.

"Wait, Cal, *Pennington*? You're the genius kid that wouldn't skip." Jocelyn smirks. "You were in my Calculus class my Senior year. Blew the fucking curve on my final exam!"

"I'm *sorry?*" I scrunch down, as she slams her mallet on a crab. Pieces going everywhere.

"You should be! It almost cost me my scholarship to The University of Pennsylvania."

"Wait, you go to UPenn?"

She smiles, sucking a bit of meat between her fingers before licking the butter off them. I think it was her trying to be sexy, but I'm more interested in what she's studying. "Yes, pre-med, pediatric oncology."

"Wow, how are the classes, I mean compared to the AP at Cradle?"

"Not so hard, but no walk in the park either. You just gotta find your groove." Jocelyn giggles touching my hand. "You know, figure out how it all fits together?"

"Right." I crack a crab, all the while I notice that Kaycee is super quiet. Well, except for the slamming of her mallet. "Kayce? You okay?"

"Yup, just chowin', you two talk. I'm gonna eat and then bounce. Jocelyn, you mind taking him home? I'll leave his bike in your flatbed."

"Wait- what?" I ask, confused.

"Just roll with it." Jocelyn smiles a smile

that makes me almost choke on my Adam's apple.

We finish eating, and she offers to split the check, which is cool. *I*, of course, was taught better and insist on taking care of it.

"Okay, but I've got dessert then."

"Um, sure? If you wanna.'

"Oh, *yeah*." She tosses her jacket over her shoulder with her purse. I notice that the top buttons on her blouse are undone, and there's a hint of white lacey bra peeking out

I have to admit she's sexy. My palms are sweaty as we get into her Chevy truck. My bike is in the back, under a tarp. We drive off, and she's really quiet, but also not going in the right direction.

"Where are we going?"

"*Dessert*." She licks her lips and reaches across the seat, stroking my thigh. "I did say it was on me."

"I- um..." We pull into an underpass that's overgrown. She stops the truck but keeps it running. Next thing I know, she's unzipping my pants! "I thought you meant Ice cream or something!"

CHAPTER 4

KAYCEE

> **Kaycee: What do you mean you didn't??**
> **Cal: Just what I said.**

I shake my head, damn near dropping the phone in the sink at work. See, I have another thing against Dunkin' Blow nuts. I work here! Have since I was sixteen. I'm middle management, that is—an assistant manager now, but it's still only part-time, and it still sucks!

I smell like sickly sweet sugar all the time, and I hate the smell of coffee now. I used to love it, used to drink it by the bucket full. Now I won't touch the stuff except when crammin' for exams.

> **Me: You know how many strings I pulled to get her down here? Uggh! You haven't had sex since Q'ira broke it off last year!**
> **Cal: I don't know her. I'm sorry. Call me later?**

I don't even answer him. I'm too annoyed. I served him up choice hottie, in a sweater set no less! What's he do with it? NOTHING! Well, not nothing, *exactly*. He did get his knob polished. At least she's not already texting me wanting to know if he's gonna call. Ugh. Boys! I swear you throw pussy in their faces, and they *still* don't know what to do with it.

I just figured she was his type, and since she was in college with a brand new truck and all daddy's money to spend, she was perfect for him and Mother Pennington the third. She wasn't someone he would have to hide. Wasn't someone like... *Me*.

***

"Hey, McLane?"

I'm in the back doing the closing shift paperwork when I hear my name. *Fucking Heath*. With a hard sigh, I come out from the little closet they call my office, and with a hand on my hip, look him up and down.

He's in fitted wranglers and a blue T-shirt that hugs his abs just right. Topped by a leather and cotton letterman's jacket. I feel my insides contract. As if my ovaries weren't already exploding.

"What? Heath?"

"You gonna get off soon?"

"That's up for some debate." I shift my weight in my stance.

"I wanna take you to get food."

"Do ya now?" I look at Mickey, my lone employee, who looks at me with a smirk.

"Yeah." He slurs it.

Fuck.

"Are you drunk?"

"I may have had a few in the parking lot with Keith and Jerome." He smirks, leaning into the counter.

"Uggh! Boys! I swear you are all toddlers!" I grab a cup and fix an Irish cream with a double turbo shot. Making it sweet so he'll drink it. "C'mon, drink this, and if after you've finished, you still wanna take me for food, I'll buy you a burger over at *Denny's*. Okay?"

He lets me lead him over to one of the tables, and I see his buddies; they're making lewd gestures and simulating sexual acts in the parking lot. I take out my phone and take a pic as Keith mounts Jerome like the dogs they are. I open the door, sending them a copy.

"This is gonna look great on my website, guys! Thanks!"

They gruff, hem, and haw.

"I suggest you beat it before I *do* post it, only I'll make sure it goes to your momma's first!"

"Skank!" Keith calls out.

"Slut!" Jerome mimics.

"You wish!" I shut the door, locking it. "The dining room is officially closed. Just drive through for the rest of the night."

Mickey nods, and I pat Heath's shoulder as I go by. He grabs my wrist, and I stop.

"They're jerks."

"Yup, and tomorrow you'll be laughin' it up with them all the same." I walk away.

An hour later and my FWB is upright and

bouncing. *Great.*

"You ready?" He asks his knees, going a million miles per hour.

"You aren't driving. We'll take the van, get some food, then I'll drop you back here."

"Killer." He gets up following me. His hand squarely on my ass as I lock the door behind me and Mickey.

"Hey! Did I say you were gettin' any? Crimson wave, *remember*?"

"And if I said I'd like to get my wings?" He whispers into my ear, making me shiver. Or maybe it was just the cold.

I lick my lips. Not moving a moment as his hands' circle to the front seam of my khaki pants.

"Night Kayce!" Mickey snickers as I'm pushed against the glass door.

"Night!" I manage, but barely for Heath's hands on me.

The parking lot is empty, except for our cars. My beat-up van and his twenty seventeen mustang convertible. Mommy and daddy bought it for him Sophomore year when he got his license. He cups me, two fingers pressing against my pussy, pushing up. His other hand goes up my shirt and under my sports bra. "Oh! Please..." I beg, breathlessly, my face pressed against the icy cold glass as he kisses my neck.

"Please, what?"

"Harder, *faster*." I pant. He doesn't disappoint.

He rubs and tweaks me until my knees go weak, and I'm a trembling mess in his arms.

Heath kisses me. "Now, how about we get that burger?"

CHAPTER 5

CALVIN

I'm so confused. I'm not sure why I didn't go for it with the sexy coed. It's not like I'm a *virgin* or a *prude*. I like sex as much as the next guy. When Q'ira and I were together, we had fun. Outdoors, food play, she even had me tie her up a few times. I wasn't really into it, but she liked it, so I obliged. I'm nothing if not an attentive lover. I listen, follow directions and body cues. Joselyn was just not... I don't know. She was everything I should want. Smart, pretty, from good breeding, and hell willing and able to suck a mean cock. I just- it was the same thing with Q'ira. We told people she broke it off, but really I had checked out on our relationship a long time before. We had been going through the motions for months. We stuck it out for our Junior Prom since the tickets had been bought and the limo rented and whatnot, but soon after, we called it for the failure it was.

Mother was disappointed, but father was glad. He didn't want as he put it, an Oriental for a daughter-in-law anyhow. They often make remarks like that. I just keep my head down and my mouth shut. What else should I do? They're my parents.

It's Friday, and because Kaycee is all about the spirit, I'm watching her as she tumbles and dances in our mascot uniform. She is Bertie the Cradle Bay Blackbird. She has got to be hot in that thing. She told me once that she only wears her skivvies inside, that it makes for better ventilation. I don't know about that. I just know she's about to fly like an eagle. The guys on the Cheer team are about to toss her like a beanbag.

She soars and spreads her *wings* showing off the red inside. Cheers all around. The game resumes, and she goes back to cheering with the girls. Though she revels in goading them and the other cheer team. She twerks and does old school dance moves complete with the coffee grinder and running man.

The game ends 42 to 53 in our favor, and the crowd goes wild. Kayce is lost to me in the crowd. Knowing she'll shower then come out, I run down to my locker for my Spanish book then make my way for the locker rooms downstairs.

I'm sitting on the stairs, as girl after girl and jock after jock come out. Where the hell is she? I go to text her.

Me: Where are u? Waiting on the stairs.

Hitting send, I hear a chirp, followed by a low laugh.

"Heath... *Stop.*" A giggle.

I tiptoe down the stairs and see Kayce leaning against the wall outside the locker room. Standing with her, all up in her personal bubble is *Heath Cramer*. I watch as he traces her blouse line into her barely-there cleavage.

"You said we could tonight. *Remember?*"

She licks those purple lips, and the blood is rushing in my head. I don't hear her response for its cacophony.

"So this is what setting me up with Miss-sucks-a-lot was about?" I seethe. I don't know why I'm so angry all of a sudden, but I can't hold it in. "You want me occupied so you can fuck the idiot jock?"

"Cal?" Kayce squirms out from under Heath and heads for me. "What are you going on for?" She's looking at me as if she hasn't completely betrayed me.

"You- you want *him*? You could have any-anyone, and you *choose him?*" I wave my hands at him in disgust

"Dude, you need to shut your trap. Or I'll do it for ya." Heath threatens.

"Ooh! The big bad jock, I've got four inches on you, and I'm not just talking about my cock!"

"You know what I tolerated you when you were doing my trig homework, but now you got a mouth." Heath pushes by Kayce.

"Stop you two." She gets between us. "Cal, calm down. What's gotten into you?" She's talking down to me like I need to be diffused. It's then I realize how tight I am. My fists, my whole body. I'm like a viper ready to strike.

All overseeing Kayce, my best friend with a guy. I swallow. "You know what? Do you. I'm gonna go do me. Take it easy."

"Cal!" Kayce calls after me, but I wrench away. I have, too; I can't have her see the pain in my eyes. I think I'm- I think...

CHAPTER 6

KAYCEE

"Forget him."

I hear Heath, but I don't look at him. Cal just flipped out on me. He grasps my arm, and I jerk away. "Get off!" I run in the direction of my best friend. I get to the bike rack; he's gone.

Fuck!

I don't think. I just hop in the van and take off down the road. Not seeing him, I assume he took through a few yards. I zip down Cooks Lane and cut back across the ravine, pulling up to his house on Bismarck drive. The van backfires. *Great.* So much for a covert showing.

I see the curtains swish, then open slightly as Missus Pennington peers out, giving me the stink eye. A few moments later, the door opens, and out comes the man of the house.

"He's not here. No use in bringing down the property value with your presence."

Of all the lousy things to say to a person. I swear somebody needs to put these pompous asshats in their place. I get out of the van, straightening all five feet three inches of me.

"Sir, I know that. I need to speak to him, though."

"Did they fight?" His wife calls from the door with a martini glass in her hand.

He raises a brow at me, and I glance at my shoes. "Seems so, snookum."

"Good, maybe I won't have to have Maria double wash his clothes anymore. It was killing the stitching in his jeans." She slams the door.

"You had better run along, little mouse. Before I have you removed for trespassing."

"You know what?" I'm suddenly grabbed, a hand over my mouth.

"I have this. Father." Cal's voice is stone cold. Like his parents.

Mister Pennington nods with a smirk to me and heads inside. It's not until he's out of earshot that I'm let go. I shove Cal.

"What the hell? Why- what?"

"Go home, Kaycee." He says defeatedly.

"I- I don't get it. Wh-what did I do?" I plead. "Is it about Heath? Why would you care? I mean, you knew I hooked up with him before. When you were with Q'ira."

"It's- doesn't matter. Just LEAVE!" He chokes out. "I don't wanna see you."

"No!" My heart races as I get into his face. "I'm not going anywhere, *Calvin*! Talk to me! Why are you being like this?"

"Like what?" He scoffs, pulling away from my hand on his arm.

"Like them!" The tears break. I'm sobbing. He barely looks at me.

"Please stop." He swallows, hard.

"I- can't. I can't lose you."

"Then why did you try so hard to shove me away?"

"I- I didn'-"

"The girl? The jock? I mean, what was next Cheerleading squad? Like for *real*? You're suddenly going for everything you and I joke on. I don't know who you're becoming. But I'm not liking it." His voice is trembling.

"Cal..." I look past him at the audience we have, I sniffle.

"Please stop crying." He looks at me finally, and I start to cough, from the mess of tears I've let myself become. His hands touch my cheeks, and he wipes at what I'm assuming is my mascara. The touch is soft and *weird.*

I grab his wrists as he's still got my cheeks cupped in his hands and is just sorta staring at me. *"Cal?"* Now I'm the one who's trembling.

CHAPTER 7

CALVIN

Counting her freckles would be like trying to count the stars. I remember trying once when we were kids. I had taken a red Crayola marker and colored in each one. I counted two hundred twenty-two before her grandpa came in and caught us. That was just on her face. She looked like she had the pox. We thought it was hilarious. Grandpa was less than thrilled.

Staring at her now, into those bird blue eyes, our childhood begins to come crashing down around us. My heart aches, my throat goes dry.

"Cal?" She says my name again, looking up at me through long lashes.

My head dips swiftly, and our lips join. I swear it's like I've been struck by lightning. All the synapses in my brain go off, telling me; *YES! This is what you want!* Her grip on my wrists tightens as I back her into the van with a thunk that breaks the kiss.

"Cal? What are you doing?" She squeaks.

"Ending our friendship." I kiss her again, this time her hands go around my neck.

She shoves me. "No! Wait! You don't get to end an argument with a kiss! Not even one like that!" She licks her lips, her fingers pressed against them. Her eyes dart back and forth. "What's going on? What are we doing?"

"I think we're evolving." I smile.

"I'm not some experiment, don't dilute me to that, Cal."

"I'm sorry. This is all new to me too. I never imagined I'd be standing in my driveway *kissing* my best friend."

"Why did you?"

"It was the only thing I could think to do. All I wanted to do at that moment, at *this* moment. Was I wrong? Fuck. What have I done?"

She looks at me with soft tearful eyes, and all I keep thinking is that I want to wrap her up in my arms and make sure I never make her cry again. "I've ruined us, haven't I? Oh, God, I have."

"Cal." Kaycee touches my hand, stopping me from my rant and pacing. "Stop. You need to let me wrap my head around this. Okay?" Her little hand touches my face making me look down and focus on her. "Just- shut up and give me a moment. *Okay?*"

I nod. Staying silent. Just watching her as her eyes seem to search. For what I'll never know. "What do you want? I mean from *this*? From *me*?"

"Reciprocation?"

Her head tilts to the side. "Have I ever *wondered*? Sure I have. I'm a red-blooded female, and you're easy on the eyes."

I push my glasses back up my face with a little grin.

"Especially when you smile like that." Her voice is but a whisper. She shakes her head. "This, though?" She points between us. "How's that supposed to work? I mean, how would we even?"

"Nothing much would change. I mean- I don't think. Why should it? We hang out all the time anyhow; it would just be... I don't know- *more*?" I close the distance she put between us. "It's a leap. I know it, but I think it might be worth it to give it a try."

"Can I think about it?"

My heart sinks, but I nod, yes. Then manage to say it. "Yeah. I mean- take all the time you need. Not like I'm going anywhere. Right?"

"Right." She smiles her hand against my chest, easing me back. "Good night, Cal." Dropping her head, she slinks by me and gets into the van. I watch her pull away before heading into the house.

CHAPTER 8

KAYCEE

Home. It's not much, but it's my safe place. Tossing the van keys into the dish on the side table, I lean against the inside of the front door and sigh.

"What's happened, my little Seabee?" Hearing my grandpa, I realize I must look like a melted mess of makeup.

I burst out laughing and tears well up again. He wheels on over to me. Grabs me and pulls me down into his lap. Wrapping my arms around him, I just start sobbing again.

"Shh, Seabee." He strokes my hair. "What's going on? Do I need to make a call?"

Anytime grandpa thinks I'm having a problem, he offers to call his old Navy buddies. He may not be able to do anything much now, but he *knows* people. Something he doesn't let us forget.

"No." I sniffle, wiping my face. He hands me a handkerchief. "Thanks." I dab my cheeks. Yup mascara and liner *everywhere*. "It's Cal."

"What happened? You have a fight?"

"Well, yes, but no. He- wants." I hesitate.

"What?"

"I think he wants to *date* me." I look up at him, and he's just got on a goofy grin. "*What?*" I whine. "Don't look at me like that then not tell me why."

"Just- we always figured *he'd* figure it out eventually."

"Figure what out?" I sound like I have a cold.

"How remarkable you actually are." Grandpa hugs me. "So, did you say yes?"

"I- I don't know what to do."

"Follow your heart, Seabee."

"I don't want to lose him, but what if it's bad? What if we're just not a good fit?"

"You two have been stuck like glue since I actually had to separate you after you glued yourselves together. I think you're compatible."

"But what *if?*"

"What if up were down and West was East? You'd adapt, you'd swing with it and roll. You'd work it out. That's what we McLane's do."

I nod but stay quiet.

"Do you love him?"

I laugh outright. "*Love?* Grandpa! I'm only eighteen, what do I know about that?"

"I *knew*. Knew it about your grandma the moment I met her. We were ten. I said I'm gonna marry that girl. And you know what?"

"You did. Took your time, but you made a life, and you traveled and saw the world together. I know Grandpa."

"Don't condescend. All I want for you girls; you *and* your mother is for you to be

29

happy. Does Cal make you happy?"

"Most days." I pout.

"That's better than some get. You go call that boy, tonight. You tell him *yes*."

"Yes, grandpa." I crawl down out of his lap and grab Stetson, my fluffy black Persian mix. He's got all the fur without the smush face. But his head has white points making it look like a hat, hence his name. With a saucer of milk for him and a meatloaf sandwich for me, I head into my room. Set up my computer and hop on Facebook. I see Cal was active a few minutes ago. Here goes nothing.

CHAPTER 9

CALVIN

There is no privacy. My parents are waiting when I go inside. To say they are displeased to hear Kayce, and I are still on speaking terms would be shortchanging it, *immensely*. Mother stays silently disgusted as Father reminds me that I am a legacy and carry a heavy name; therefore, I should have a bit more thought about who I spend my time with. I just yes, Sir him and go to my room.

I surf the net, check out a few sites. Web programming, design, and stuff. I look into the programs at UPenn. I really am leaning toward Submatriculation, which would allow me to get my BA and JD at the same time. Yeah, so I'm looking at Law like daddy wants. I want to actually help people. I start going through my email. My Facebook starts to ring. It's Kayce.

I hit the answer button as I'm skimming my spam folder. I spy something from Pennsylvania State University. I'm quiet, and the look on my face must be something because Kayce is all up in the call.

"Cal? What's wrong? What's the matter?

Is everything okay?"

"I- um, I got an email..."

"Yeah. Okay."

"No, I mean, I got an *e-mail.*"

Her eyes pop as she registers what I'm saying. The schools, they don't mail the fat envelopes anymore, they send simple electronic correspondence now. Mine happens to have wound up in my spam. It also looks to have been *read*. My fucking parents. Probably my mother. Came in *cleaning* and went through my shit—*again*.

"Cal? Read it."

"I- I'm- What if it says no?"

"What if it says *yes?*"

I click the button to read the message.

"Dear Mister Pennington, We are pleased to inform you..." I stop my eyes scanning the rest as Kayce is jumping up and down, squealing happily. "I got it. I fucking got in." I can't believe what I'm seeing. I mean, I knew I could, but to *actually* do?

"Then, I guess you got two bits of good tonight." Kayce says, finally calming.

I glance at her; she is fresh-faced, in a tank, and if my peripheral vision from her jumping, was correct, a pair of little shorts.

"Yes."

I tilt my head. *"Yes?"*

"Yes, you dolt. To our conversation earlier. Let's do this; try it on for size. See how we fit."

I smile. "I would really like that."

"Good, so I'll see you tomorrow after I get out of work, swing by the house. We can hang out. Grandpa's going to the Lodge, and mom's got a double at Denny's."

"Sounds good, should I bring anything? A bucket of chicken? Snacks, movies?"

"All that. Oh, and *condoms*."

I look at her, stunned as she wiggles her fingers at me, grins then hangs up.

***

Today has been *strange*. I'm on cloud nine but can't really show it. My parents would find a way to destroy all my happiness if I did. I called the DMV and made an appointment to take the driver's exam again. I'm pretty sure I'll pass it this time as I took six practice exams and passed *all* of them. If I'm going to be going to Pennsylvania, I'm gonna need transportation. If I take out a small loan for school, I can afford to dip into my college fund for a car. The cold is coming back, so much to my chagrin, I'm having to Uber it around before going to Kaycee's house. I run the tab on the emergency credit card.

I'm in Walmart, having taken a ride out to New Castle. It's the only place I could get all the things I needed for today. They have a food center, so the chicken was even doable. I also got potato wedges and cheese curds cause I know Kaycee loves them. Along with a four-pack of California Raspberry Coke. Another of Kaycee's likeables. For snacks, we have redvines, chocolate reisen, gummy bears, and of course, popcorn with extra movie theater butter.

I pick up the remake of *Fahrenheit 451*,

an adaptation of a book of the same name by Ray Bradbury. It's Sci-fi, but it's also got a deeper message. About man, and what happens when we lose touch with each other to only focus on technology. It may have been written in the early twentieth, but the man knew some shit.

I'm standing in the sexual wellness section, you know, right next to the tampons? Guess it's better than at CVS, where it's next to the pregnancy tests! I mean, if you need one, you don't usually need the other, am I right?

I've never bought condoms. When Q'ira and I were having sex, she took care of that. I just had to put them on. There are so many kinds, Trojan, SKYN, LifeStyles, Durex. Everyone has a pleasure pack of some kind. *Flavors?* Just eww. Then there's latex-free. If she needed those, she'd have said. *Right?* I'm thinking anything that says Fire is bad and anything too thin, not good either. I sigh and just take a pack of LifeStyles Ultra-Sensitive. They say it's like being bare. I wouldn't know. I get to the register and am sure I'm fifty shades of red.

"Have a nice night." The girl that rings me out giggles as I take my bags. Yup red as an apple.

Getting to Kaycee's, I'm nervous as all fuck. I swear I wasn't this on edge when Q'ira and I had sex the first time. Though it was kinda sprung on me. Or rather, *she* sprang on me. It was sloppy and short-lived, to say the least. Though according to her, I had a great recovery time. I also eventually, improved.

I take a deep breath and knock. She opens the door in yoga pants and a thick cable knit sweater down to her mid-thigh.

"Hey." She lets me in, and I notice there is a roaring fire.

"Sorry, it's a bit cold. The oil tank is, well- empty. So it's just the fireplace and a space heater right now."

"It's fine; we'll build a fort, then we can watch the movie." I hold up my bags.

"I'll just put this in the oven then. You know where the linens are."

I nod. We used to build forts in the living room all the time. We'd have competitions and see who could withstand more nerf gun attacks. I was usually the loser. Somehow her's were always more structurally sound.

I grab the sheets and ropes plus a few nails and a hammer. Being taller than four feet now has its advantages. I suspend ropes and tie up the sheets, making us a fine canopy with the space heater at its source and the fire at the other end. Making a nicely heated environment. I pull all the pillows off the couch into the floor and cover them with blankets.

"Here." Kaycee hands me LED twinkle lights.

"Nice touch." I smile, taking them. I'm crawling around when I feel hands wrap around me. I freeze. Her hands grab my T-shirt and lift it up. I sink down so she can get it over my head. Kaycee kisses my back between the shoulder blades.

"Relax." She whispers. "It's just me. You

trust me." I feel her press herself against me and realize as I'm grazed by hard nipples that she's taken off the sweater.

Swallowing, I feel her leaving feather-light kisses down my back. She pushes me forward. I lay on my stomach, and she's rubbing me down, her bouncy curls trailing across my exposed skin.

"You can turn over if you want to." Kayce whispers, she's kneeling between my legs, so I'm careful not to kick her. Rolling, I see she's in just a pair of boy shorts that sit low on her hips. In her belly button is a steel rod with an adorable little pink butterfly.

I narrow my eyes. "When did *that* happen?"

"This?" She smiles, fingering it playfully. "A few months ago. I didn't say nothing cause I know you would have yelled."

"It's just I don't see the attraction to driving metal through one' s body." She's got a pouty look on her face. "Though it is cute."

"Thanks." She arches her back, squaring her shoulders. Her small but firm breasts perk up. "So, are you going to come here, or shall I come to you?"

CHAPTER 10

KAYCEE

Courage girl. I'm a ball of nerves, but I can't let him see. If he sees- this won't happen. I'm already half-naked; there's really no going back. Honestly? I'm pretty sure I've wanted this for a while. I never liked Q'ira, and thinking on it, I think this is why. *I* wanted to be the one under the covers with him.

Crawling up his legs, I straddle him. We have time; there's no need to rush this. It's one of the perks to a single-parent family. A lot of alone time.

He grasps my hips firmly, and I smile, bending down to kiss him. I know that I said he was like a brother to me, but it's nothing like kissing a brother would be. I can feel my arousal pooling in my panties as I move up and down on him. Well hello! I'm met with a hard cock through jeans. I jump as this surprises me. I laugh, as does he.

"Sorry, but you are sorta rubbing on it." Cal chuckles.

Reaching down between us, I caress him. *"Now,* I'm rubbing on it."

He gasps. "Yup." He chokes a bit as I go

to kiss him again. His hands slip up my back, and he pulls me down, rolling us across the floor, so he's got the top position.

"Oh? You think so?" I open my legs, lifting them to give him space to settle between them.

"Is this okay?"

"C'mere." I grab his face. We kiss more, but he keeps his hands to himself. I have to fish for them, bringing them to my breasts. Once he's got the handful, he's got the moves. Gentle squeezes, playful flicks to my nipples. Breaking our kisses, he moves down with his mouth. "Oh!" Slips from me loud enough, Stetson answers with a yowl.

That, of course, has us sputtering.

"I'm sorry." I'm bouncing all over from laughing. "This was *not* how I imagined it."

"Me either. But I think, the yowler aside, it's perfect. Why's it gotta be all serious? I mean, why not have fun? Laugh a bit?" Cal says, his fingers tracing my shorts.

I suck my lip into my mouth. "I can do *fun*." I pull him back up. I'm not quite there yet. Besides, I need to know what I'm dealing with. If that pop up is any indication, he wasn't just boasting about the extra four inches on Heath.

I know I said we'd showered together since puberty, but that was still a few years and like two growth spurts for him ago. He and I settle on our sides, sinking into the pillows as we go back to making out. Casually I trail my hands to his waist, unbutton his jeans and slide my hand down into them. I don't have to go far before I've got rock hard cock in my hand.

"Christ." I blurt nervously.

"What? Is something wrong?"

"Um, n-no." He's gonna split me like wood.

"Kayce?" He stops, stops kissing me, panting in my ear.

"No, we're- we're good." I start to rub up and down his length. My thumb slipping over the head. Now it's him moaning and trying to mount me again. I let him; it makes this easier.

"That's- it feels *so* good," Cal whispers heavily before sucking my nipple into his mouth. The sensation mixed with him humping me has me on fire. The little fort is like a sauna, and my scent is filling it.

"I need you to prep me a bit; you're a lot bigger than I'm used to." I sigh in stops and starts.

He rolls, stops me, then rolls us again, getting us back to our sides. Demolishing my mouth again, he starts to work me over with his hand. Slipping his middle finger between my freshly shaved lips.

"Fuck, you're soaked." He laughs, fishing around.

"A little higher there, Cal."

He curls his finger back, hitting my clit. "Here?"

I rise up. "Mmm-hmm." He flicks it a few times before venturing further south. He pushes his fingers into me, and I whimper. Then pant as he bangs at my insides. Hard, and fast. Grabbing his wrist, I slow him. "It's not a race. In this game, we both get to finish.

I promise."

"Sorry."

"Don't apologize, just take off your pants."

He smiles and easing away from me does as I ask. That bike and his boxing classes have really paid off. Not only has he got great abs, but his thighs are like corded wood. Christ, I could chew on them for days. I pull off my now sticky shorts and go for the box of condoms I found in the bags with the food.

His marvelous cock does its little dance, and I laugh a smidge, as he chuckles. "This guy's happy to see you."

"It would seem that way. Now let's get him dressed." I tear open the package and hand him the little rubber barrier that means the difference between freedom and getting stuck in this shit town. I watch as he fumbles with and drops the thing. "Well, we now know why you don't play football. *Butterfingers!*" I get up on my knees and kissing him roll the thing down over his throbbing cock. "Since I had to do the work, I may as well reap the benefits." I push him down and climb on to him. Heath never let me be on top. It was always from the back or him on me. This was going to be fun.

I grasp him as he grips my hips again and leading him to the sweet spot, I sit, taking him into me. I'm filled up, and just when I think I can't take anymore, he thrusts, and I'm hit even deeper. I have to lean into him, taking him at the angle. He clutches my ass and lifts me up, then lets me drop. Hard, solid strokes. A few of these and I'm beyond my limit. I'm moaning and bouncing on his cock, as I come. He flips us and dives down into me. Faster. I rotate my hips to match him thrust for unforgivable thrust. Reaching down, I start to rub my clit and bring myself over again. I like to come and will do what I need to, to make that happen, *often*. Getting my cue, he pulls out. Leaving me feeling empty until he buries his head in my pussy. Replacing cock with tongue.

I squeal, coming instantly.

"Seabee! I'm home!"

"Fuck!" I say, and Cal's head pops up, hitting the top of the fort, he's tangled in the lights. "Oh, no!" I can't help but laugh even as I panic. I pull my sweater over my head. It'll cover everything, at least. Rushing out of the fort as Cal tries to get dressed, I head to the front door to catch Grandpa.

"You got company?" He asks as I kiss his cheek, helping him into the house. His driver Boyd having gotten him this far. His electric chair nearly runs over my bare feet.

"Just Cal."

He raises an eye. "Where is he, and where are your *pants*?"

"Well?" I shrug.

"Go put on some pants, girl."

"Yes, grandpa." I drop my head and go for my room.

CHAPTER 11

CALVIN

I felt like Uncle Fester, tangled in a tuna net. By the time I come crawling out of the fort, I am nose to chrome with Grandpa Compton's wheelchair. I swallow as the man looks down his nose at me.

"Busted." He says calmly. "You may as well finish coming out, boy." He backs up to allow me an exit.

"Thank You. Sir." I swallow, standing as he is staring at me. *Hard.* Staring at my pants in particular. I look down and realize that there's a bit of the condom wrapper sticking out of my pocket. "Shit," I whisper.

"*Yeah...* Shit. Seabee! Get your ass out here!" Grandpa Compton shouts sternly. "You? *Sit.*" He points to the dining room chairs behind him.

I slink over and down into the chair I go as Kayce comes out in Pj's bottoms and her sweater. "Yeah, Grandpa What-?" She stops seeing the look on me; I'm sure.

"You and this boy?" He asks. "You messing 'round in *my* house?"

"Grandpa, we- I'm sorry."

"You should be. You said he wanted to date, *not* compromise you."

She chuckles at the phrasing.

"This is no laughing matter. Your momma was your age when you were born. She thought she was being careful too." He points to me. "Condoms break, moments of lust lead to broken promises *and* babies."

"I know grandpa, I'm sorry. We just..."

"You just nothing. I thought I taught you better." He looks at me. "What have you got to say for yourself, *Calvin*?"

"I love her." It slips out of my mouth before I even realize what I've said. Her eyes bug out of her head. Grandpa Compton looks less surprised.

"Love doesn't pay bills or put food in her belly. Your family isn't going to care that you *love* her."

"I-" What was I gonna say? Sure I love her, but I don't know if she loves me the same way. We only just started and already, he wants me to make declarations?

"You two need to be smarter. You have so many opportunities. Don't waste them for a little thing like sex."

"Yes, grandpa."

"Yes. Sir."

"Now, did I see a chicken bucket?"

"Calvin brought food. Snacks and a movie." Kayce says, breaking the tension.

"Well, let's hop to it. Seeing as you two need a chaperone."

***

Kayce kisses me as she drops me off down the road from my house. It's been a decent night, blue balls and all. I don't want an argument with my parents to ruin it.

"Go to prom with me?" I ask as I'm getting out.

"Cal. You know I hate those formal dances."

"*Please*. We'll get you a gorgeous dress; you can go to the salon. I know you like having mani-pedis when you can scrape for it."

"I can't afford it."

"Did I ask you to afford it? I asked you to go; I'll foot the bill."

"I can't let you do that."

"We'll work it out. Coffee till prom." I slap the hood. "I won't take no for an answer."

She just nods with a huge grin as she pulls away, the van backfiring.

I head into the house to find my mother standing at the foot of the stairs. My sister Caryn on the couch. She's apparently down to make me miserable. She's just as stuck up as my parents; only she tends to have zero boundaries.

"Hey, little bro. Hear you applied to UPenn. You tryin' to get away?"

"Caryn." I say as mother narrows her eyes at me.

"You were with that McLane girl again."

"Yes, mother." I don't lie to them, I may try to not tell them everything, but if asked outright, I don't ever lie. What would be the point?

"Ugh!"

Caryn gets up. "Haven't you gotten over that piece of trash yet?"

"I only see one piece of trash, *Caryn.*"

"Calvin, you apologize!" Mother demands.

"Why? She can insult my girlfriend, but I can't point out the obvious?"

"*Girlfriend?*" Caryn sniffs. "Eew, I thought I smelled low rent punani." She waves her hand in the air. "You should really shower, Lord, knows what you picked up in that van or God forbid that house!?"

I go to grab her, and Mother steps in. "You need an attitude adjustment. *Calvin.* We're cats; they're mice. *Vermin.* You can play with it, but if you don't eat it fast, you're going to wind up with *fleas*. Or worse *worms.*" She rotates her wrist. "You, my dear, are simply infested and in need of a good dipping." She grabs me by the head, trying to drag me to the mudroom.

A year ago, I would have wound up in the garden shower, as she scrubbed at me with a pumice stone. It wouldn't have been for the first time. This time I wrench out from her grip, losing some hair in the process.

"Let me go, you fucking harpy!" I bat at her hands.

She looks at me, wounded. "How did I give birth to a child that would dare talk to me like that? I should have never brought you into this world."

"Yes, yes, we know I was shit out to appease him!" I point up the stairs at my now watching father. "How many times will I have to fucking hear that? You all posture, preen, and act like you are untouchable. *Why?* Because we have fucking money?" I roar. "You're all bigots. Despicable people. You call *them* vermin? Then I suppose I am too! So put me out of my God damned misery. Please! Take out your claws and tear me up, before I infest you too." My mother goes to smack me, and I catch her hand. "There will be no more of that either. I'm a grown man and will no longer be dictated to by you, or any bitch in this house who thinks that they know better. You *women*. You think that just because you spread your legs either to have us or to get us, you can dictate what we think, look at or who we *love*? That's bullshit. Men have feelings! *I* have feelings! I'm not just the nice kid down the road. I'm a man. One that's turning eighteen in a couple of weeks. At that point, you can't stop me from doing or seeing anyone I choose. So suck it up, buttercup. Maybe you should go do something useful, like make me a fucking sandwich! I'll keep seeing and fucking whomever I choose, and that includes Kaycee McLane. If you or anyone else doesn't like, you can take a fucking hike right back to the kitchen!" I push her hand away, and she tries to hit me again. I push her back I don't mean to hit as hard as I do, but I'm so angry. She trips on the stairs and falls.

Father is right there. "Get out. Do you think you're a fucking man? Then make something of yourself."

"Fine!" I go to head up the stairs to my room, and he cuts me off.

"You go with what's on your back. You

don't want to be one of us? Then why should you get to keep what I've paid for?"

"I'm getting my school stuff."

He sucks his teeth.

"Let him, *Calvin.*" Mother says from her defeated spot on the floor.

I run upstairs. Packing up my school stuff, including my laptop. Finding my sculpture of Ben Franklin, my covert way of supporting the University of Pennsylvania's Mascot, the Quaker. See, my sister is an idiot and doesn't know the difference between UPenn and Pen State. Anyway, Ben was a gift from my Uncle Douglas before he moved to New York. What mother didn't know was his head comes off, and I've been stashing cash in him since I started doing summers at the Cradle Bay yacht club. Father wanted me to learn what it was like to have to *earn* my money so I would get the idea out of my head that I was built for anything other than family money.

Boy was he pissed when I *liked* working. I like people, and people like me, so they tipped. *Well.* I take the lion and getting everything into my bag breeze by the people who call themselves my family.

Getting on my bike, I ride, to where I'm not sure yet.

CHAPTER 12

KAYCEE

Grandpa didn't rat me out. Though he has made me promise that if Cal and I are going to have sex that it not be in his living room or on his furniture. That includes his pillows. I, of course, agree and apologize again, finally going to bed with a smile. It wasn't a complete disaster.

It's about five o'clock when my phone chirps. Some message on Facebook. I try to ignore it, but then my Instagram dings too. Followed by more and more chirps. Tossing off the blanket, I grab the phone. Unlocking it, I see a message from Taylor Holmes. One of the cheerleaders I sorta talk to.

Taylor: *Have you seen this?*

I click the video, and it's a remix of Cal. He's screaming at his mother. It pauses and rewinds over and over with industrial pop music playing in the background over him, saying, *Fucking Kaycee McLane*. In that cut and mix way, that sounds like a stutter over the word fucking.

Me: WTH?

I send back.

Taylor: It's all over the place. Plus, some really rank shit he said about women. I didn't know he was such a pig.
Me: He's not.
Taylor: Yeah. You would defend him, now wouldn't you?
Me: What's that supposed to mean?

No response, she even goes offline. *Bitch.* I sit up and scroll to find Cal's messages. I hit the call button. I don't care if I wake him.

"Hello?" His voice is gruff.

"You need to start talking. What happened?"

"How'd you- know what doesn't matter. I'm gone."

"What are you going on about? Have you seen the videos? You told them we had *sex*?"

"I- wait-what video?" I hear movement. "Fucking Caryn."

"Your *sister*?"

"She was home when I got in; I had a really bad fight with her and mother. It was- let's just say I'm over at the Mayflower."

"The rat motel over on Cherry Street? Ugh, why didn't you call me?"

"For what?"

"Room number."

"Twelve."

"Get dressed."

I pull myself together, and in fifteen, I'm ripping him out of the hooker haven.

"C'mon." I demand, shoving him down the walkway.

"Where are we going?"

"Right now, to get some breakfast, seeing as I'm up at the ass crack of dawn."

***

Denny's. An American late-night tradition. It's also where mom works, meaning I get free food. We walk in, and I see Michelle one of the servers. "Mom, busy?"

"I think she's in the back, go have a seat, I'll grab her. You want a Chocolate Peanut Butter shake?"

I nod.

"Calvin?"

"Same." He says, pushing up his glasses.

We go sit across from each other in a booth and wait. My mom, like me, is middle management. She's taking online and in-person classes over at Wilmington University. She hopes to get promoted to store or even district manager once she finishes.

"Why are we here?" Calvin asks as the shakes are delivered.

"To talk to my mom. Dummy."

Out comes my mom, but the smile on her face falls when she sees Cal. Slipping her phone into her pocket, she shakes her head. Damnit, she knows.

"Honey. *Calvin.*" She looks uncomfortable.

"Mom. You got a couple?"

She looks at him again. He looks like someone kicked his favorite puppy.

"Yeah." Grabbing a chair, she sits at the head of our little table. Typically she would slip in next to me. "You want to explain this? Explain why my daughter's name is falling from your sewer mouth?"

"It's all my sister, Tracie. I swear I didn't mean it the way it's being said. It's all out of context. She cut out where mother *grabbed* me. *Threatened* me. The horrible things she said about you guys. About Kayce."

"Words, Cal. You laid your hands on your momma. Knocked her down."

"An Accident. One I've been thrown out of the house for committing."

Her head nods slowly as she looks at me. "Hence, your five-thirty appearance. You want us to put him up?"

"Mom, he was staying in the Mayflower."

"We can't have that, now can we? Though what happened to the young man from earlier this week? I thought you were seeing him? Now you and Calvin are an item?" Mom sounds confused.

"It's complicated." I answer.

"I bet. I'll allow it." She puts up her hand. "But I'm trusting you, both of you. I know you're old enough to make your own bad decisions. Just *please* try and make better ones than the adults in your lives."

"Thank you, Tracie." Cal says, and she pats his shoulder.

"Get some food in you, you may as well hang around for shift change, so you can just

bring me home too."
"You got it, mom."

CHAPTER 13

CALVIN

What the hell am I gonna do? I'm sitting in Kayce's kitchen, looking at her mom Tracie, and her Grandpa Compton. Kayce couldn't get a replacement on short notice, so she's gone to work.

"So they've had an eventful eighteen or so hours." Grandpa Compton says, looking from Tracie to me. "Well, boy, if you're gonna stay, you gotta earn your keep."

"Absolutely, Sir." I agree. What else am I gonna do?

"You'll have chores. Shoveling if there's snow, cleaning the gutters out after the thaw. *Yard work.* You'll be expected to go to school, to keep your grades up. We don't take to slackers."

"Of course. Sir."

"Where's your stuff?"

"This is it. Just my school stuff, laptop, and what I'm wearing."

"Christ. Trace, this kids not even got himself a clean pair of shorts." He squirms in his chair.

"I have money, a little over two thousand

dollars."

"You're gonna need it. In the meantime, I may have some things that will do. C'mon, Calvin." Tracie interrupts me.

I look at her curiously as she leads me into the basement. "Um- if you're gonna kill me, make it fast." I mumble on the rickety stairs.

Tracie laughs. "No, Calvin. But I do have some things that Logan left behind."

Logan was Kaycee's dad. He left when she was two. She pulls out an unmarked tote.

"I knew there was a reason I held on to this stuff. You never know when you're gonna need something." She half-smiles. "You're a thirty-two twenty-eight?"

"Twenty-nine, but I can sling low."

"The jeans will fit." She holds up a pair of dark blue jeans. "Here have it, whatever you want, bring it up. I'll run it through the wash. When you're done, we'll go out to the Mall in Newark, get you some underthings, toiletries, and whatnot."

"Thank you."

"You can thank me by *not* making me a grandmother."

"I will, er, rather I won't."

She nods and heads back upstairs.

***

"I can't believe you *actually* went shopping. With my mom!" Kayce teases as she sits in a towel, drying her voluminous curls. Most of the time, she straightens her hair, but when she's home, it's curly. I love her curls, though.

"Hey, why do you always straighten it? Your hair. I mean."

"I dunno, because I look like a fucking poodle otherwise."

"You really don't, though." I get up, taking the blow dryer away. "Think we could try it out? You know- let them see the you, I get to see?"

She looks up at me through the mirror, and I see her visibly swallow when I touch her. She lowers the towel exposing her naked little body to me. "Lock the door." She whispers.

I go over and lock the door, then come back to her. I'm about to lift her up when she stops me. "Just enjoy the vis." She smiles as she grabs my waistband and unzips me. A few strokes of her hand, and I'm getting hard. Then she does it, licks me from balls to tip. I shudder as she bathes me in sweet saliva. I reach out, cupping a breast, tweaking her nipple as she starts to suck me off.

She goes down as far as she can and jerks the rest of me, making sure every inch of my cock is gaining equal attention.

"That feels..." I lose my train of thought as I watch her head slide back and forth, lubing up my piston. Grabbing my ass, she pulls me closer as I feel her swallow and stick a finger up my ass! "Fuck."

"Easy, you're *really* gonna like this." She says, popping off me. Pressing up on that space between my ass and my balls, she makes me see stars. I almost lose my footing and drop back against her vanity as she gobbles down my cock and keeps at me with her fingers. I feel my balls get heavy; I'm gonna come soon.

"Kayce, I'm gonna- come."

She nods and sucks harder, digs in deeper. Kayce keeps going even after I come. Sucking, fingering, it gets me hard again fast.

I'm still in a haze from coming, when she speaks, popping candy in her mouth. "Fuck me." Getting off me, then standing, she grabs my hand and pulls me to the bed. By the time I get out of my pants, she's got the condom ready. "I want you to make me crumble."

"*How?*" I ask. I know I've done this, but I've never made a girl *crumble*. Come once or twice, sure. But she's asking for miracles on limited experience.

"Get on the bed. *Kneel.*" I listen. "I'm gonna get on you, hold me up, you can do that?"

I nod as she strokes me, making sure I stay good and hard. Getting her legs on either side of me, she squats over my cock. I grab her ass, and she guides me inside. She's tight and warm. Her kiss is sweet and fruity from the candy. Rising up and down on me, I moan into her mouth as we catch a rhythm, and I start to lift her, letting her slide up and down me. Her arms wrap my shoulders, and her eyes lock with mine. I go to kiss her.

"Keep your eyes open. Stay here, *with* me." She pants.

I avert my eyes. "It's weird."

"You love me? You said it. So connect with me. Not just my hot wet pussy." She kisses me, and I keep contact. Feeling like a silvery river is washing over me, and she's my life raft. My thighs are as slick as her back, as I lower her to the blanket, getting a new perspective. I watch as she leans back, seeing myself as I enter her again, and again. It's fucking hot. Like interactive porn.

The room is filled with the vapor and smell of our sex, as we finish. I get rid of the condom, and she opens the window to air us out. She scoots under the covers, so I join her back on the bed.

"You okay?" I ask her as she wipes a tear from her cheek.

"Yeah." She looks at me, then kisses me. "I- think- I love you too." Kayce says her lips millimeters from mine.

"Well, that makes things more interesting." I smile as she lays her head on my chest.

CHAPTER 14

KAYCEE

Monday comes, and with it, the dog and pony show. That *lying* little video? Well, it went fucking viral. Cal's friend's list has been cut by more than half, and those that have stuck around are divided. To some, asshole boys, he's a hero. To others, the female populace, he's the devil's own. He's gotten anonymous threats and everything. In less than twenty-four hours, Cal has gone from everybody's BFF to public enemy numero uno. We get to the school and are given a wide berth as we go inside. Whispers, snickers. I kiss him as we part till lunch and get hissed at.

"Oh, grow up!" I snap. "If you actually believe that wasn't edited for cheap thrills!"

Cal grabs me. "Kayce, just don't engage."

I nod. He kisses me again, and we get hit with a cup of hot coffee!

"Pig!" Shouts a girl that I've never even seen before.

"Ugh!" I squeal. As I'm pulled back by Cal. He drags me into the bathroom. My face stings. He locks the door. Then strips off my drenched top. Soaking it in the sink with cold water, he pats my face with it.

"Shit, this is gonna be red for a while."

"Yeah, they don't put a caution on them cups for nothing." I cry. The tears sting the burns. A knock comes to the door.

Cal hesitates.

"It's Ciera, Cummings. I have some ice and clean t-shirts for you both."

Ciera is in our seventh-period Spanish class. She's tutored Cal for the last year. He may be a core class genius, but he's got no tongue for language.

He rushes over and lets her in, locking the door behind her. "Next, it'll be fire and pitchforks." He spits. "Tell me you don't believe that the way it shows."

Ciera shrugs. "I mean, I've never heard you talk that way, but it *was* you. *You* did *say* those things."

"To one person about her and my cunty sister who was, by the way, the uploader of this little fucked movie. She's a film student at NYU. Who conveniently didn't record my Harpy mother calling everyone without their kind of money vermin, and flea-ridden. Likened them to playthings that should be eaten fast."

"You said some really putrid things."

"I was *angry*." Cal ices my cheek and his chest. He's red as a lobster in splotches. I'm afraid to check my face.

"Delia Hemerling was grabbed by the security guard that saw it happen. She's been taken to the office, and they are waiting out there for you two." Ciera explains, plainly.

"I just want to go home and curl back up in bed with you," I say as I lean toward him and he holds me against his icy chest.

"So that *was* a kiss in the hallway? You two are together?"

I feel Cal nod.

"Well, shit. Okay. Explains a few things."

I look at her.

"That Delia chick had a crush on you."

She looks at me.

"*Me?*"

'She knew you were Bertie. Got enamored, I guess the video of *him* saying he was fucking you got her upset."

"Ya think?" Cal condescends.

"Just get clothes on and let 'em take you to the office. You're gonna have to decide if you're pressing charges. This was assault after all."

"Yeah. Thanks." We take the T-shirts from her; they are just plain white T's.

"From Mister Mackey, the art and design teacher. They're doing silk screening this semester."

I nod at Ciera, pulling it on. I hop off the sink counter. "Guess we're facing the firing squad and giving up *all* our privacy."

CHAPTER 15

CALVIN

I'm a pariah. The females in this school have spent the day leering at me and my favorite teacher, Miss Warner, during fifth when she did roll call even skipped saying my name. Just nodded and kept going. It makes my heart ache to think that these people, people who have known me my entire life believe that I'm really like that. They believe that I'm some sort of sociopathic monster that beats his mother. If they had any idea the torture, I've endured at their hands.

I remember being ten and coming home late from playing with Kayce. I'd hit a curb wrong and flipped my bike. Went head over heels. Busted up my rim and cut up my arms and my knee. I was only late because I had to walk the bike the rest of the way with a limp. Mother? She didn't care; I was making her late for a dinner party. She beat the hell out of me with her silver-plated hairbrush. You know the ones with the big wide, flat backs? It wasn't until after when she saw the blood that she even bothered to ask me what happened. Then she just told me not to get blood on the carpet. She left, and it was our housekeeper at the time, Amelia, who patched me up. Fed me and put me to bed.

It was *always* like that. *Always* about *them*. What I do is a direct reflection on them. Well, they can have credit for this one, it was them coming out of me after all.

I meet Kayce in the hallway just outside the café, and she looks like she could fall asleep on her feet.

"Hey? What's up?" I say, taking her bag as it slips off her shoulder toward the floor.

"I'm exhausted from turning the other cheek all day." She whimpers. "You know what happens when you turn the other cheek? They smack that one too, with these burns, it really hurts."

"I'm sorry that you are going through this because of me."

"No, *we're* going through this because people are assholes." Kayce slips her arm into mine, making me look down at her curiously.

"What? Is the PDA too much?"

"No, I just didn't think *you* would be into it." I answer gently as we hover at the café entrance. "We usually make fun of those other couples that get mushy in public."

"Yeah, well, never had a reason to be like that. I do now." She squeezes my hand, and we walk into the wolf's den.

You could hear a pin drop as we grab our trays and get in line. Stares. Glares and leers. We turn, and the whole room seems to turn back on, only it's filled with whispers. I see Heath Cramer and his lackeys as we pay for the crappy food.

"Hey, tough guy. You like hitting on women, huh?" Heath looks Kayce up and down. "Was that what I was doing wrong, honey? I didn't smack ya around enough?" He snickers. "You really *are* a skanky ho."

Before I can stop her, Kayce is in his face. "Yeah? I'm a ho? Well, that just goes to show you for the cow shit you are. Seeing as you loved it while I was digging my fingers into your ass!" She laughs. "Would you like me to share the video I got of you with my *former* dildo up your crack while you jerk off- you fucking perv?"

"I- uh-"

"Dude, *really*?" Jerome asks, laughing. "You bouncing on rubber cocks now?"

People start to laugh. She's got command of the room. "Oh, now you laugh? Is this entertainment? You are all fucking SHEEP!"

"Kayce?" I grab her as she starts bleating at them. Christ. What have I done to her? Mother said she'd ruin me, but it seems I'm ruining her. "Hey. Calm down." I demand as she wrenches away from me outside.

"Ugh! I'm just so sick of these losers and their hoity-toity attitudes! They act like they never made a mistake."

"It's been twenty-four hours. Give it time. It'll blow over." I pull her to me, doing that little sway thing people do during a big hug. She settles against me with a huge sigh. "What if it doesn't?"

"And what if we had hands for feet?" She purses her lips, glaring at me. "My point is, does it really matter? We got just short of four months, and we're done."

"Speaking of which, when is your appointment to go up to the campus?"

"Next week, after I pass my driver's exam and buy a car."

"Oh-wait what?" She asks, confused as Triply, the pervy security guard rounds the corner.

"Hey, you two, back to class. We've had enough crazy from you for one day."

Kayce and I skip going back to the lunchroom and instead spend the rest of the period making out and groping in the back of the van.

CHAPTER 16

KAYCEE

The past week has been hell. The teasing and the bastardization of that video keep popping up. Somebody on the online newspaper is being a fucker because it's showed up there on the school's official website. No sooner does IT take it down than a new, improved one goes up. They're threatening to take the site down entirely. So much for my one extracurricular. I liked the paper. Writing about the games from an insider perspective. *Bertie's Head Games* was popular too. I wear a small camera on the mascot uniform and video the game and the crowd. It was my college essay. Sadly I've no money for school. Even with scholarships or loans, there's just not enough to really send me anywhere but the local community college.

I'm sitting in the waiting area at the DMV reading *Fahrenheit 451*, by Ray Bradbury. The movie was really good, so I wanted to compare notes. It's different, the political issues are a little more in your face in the book, but that's not a *bad* thing. Cal passed the written driver's exam and is now out doing the driving part. I'm glad they use their own cars here at the DMV, as I don't think the van would have been cleared for it.

I glance up and see him smiling, shaking the instructor's hand. I lock my phone, standing as he comes inside.

"I got it!" He's so excited he picks me up, giving me a half swing.

"Okay, you crazy fox, put me down, go get your picture done so we can go. I'm *starving*."

Cal kisses me, and off he goes. I know I am supposed to be all happy for him, but this just makes things harder. I was gonna lose him. I knew that he was going to go away to school. But now... Now that we've started up something, how do I say goodbye?

After this, he wants to close the deal on a '03 Santa Fe he found in Delaware City. Mom is having him added to our insurance, so that will help him. Everything is just happening so fast. Our coupledom, his acceptance to UPenn, this disaster of our reputations. I'm feeling stretched really thin all of a sudden. Like the walls are closing in on me, and I can't find the release button on the damn escape hatch.

CHAPTER 17

CALVIN

Kaycee has been quiet. I know that she's stressing over what's going on at school. I'm not so good either; I just hide it better. We've gotten through it, though. My teachers are still shunning me, but whatever. I do the work; I know the material. When finals come, I'll blow the curve as always. I've got no time for petty. We're in the stretch, and this weekend is about the future. Kaycee and I are going out to Philadelphia, Pennsylvania, to check out my soon to be college and home for the next four years. I'm excited, and nothing is gonna bring me down.

Top it off; it's my eighteenth birthday, Sunday. With that comes a bit of freedom. I'll be able to buy the car I have on hold, with cash, and I'll no longer be beholden to anyone, but me. The van is packed, and Kaycee is in her traveling clothes. That is to say yoga pants and a cozy sweater. Tracie was in tears this morning when the oil company came and made a delivery. Hey, if I'm gonna stay with the McLane's, I'm gonna help take care of them as much as they take care of me. I even got a nod from Grandpa Compton.

"Now you got all your warm stuff? It's supposed to drop into the low thirties this weekend." Tracie says, concerned, watching as I toss two duffle bags into the back of the van.

"Yes, mom." Kaycee drones. "I'm only gonna be gone for two days. Take a chill pill."

Tracie hugs her. "Be good, stay safe." She looks at me. I know that look. It's the don't do anything stupid look.

"Love you, mom. Bye, Grandpa."

"Have fun, Seabee." He waves as we get the van started.

"You ready?" Kaycee asks.

"Been waiting for this all my life." I grasp her hand. "Not at all. But I got you, so I can weather it all."

She squeezes my hand and then lets me go so she can drive. One hour and three bathroom breaks, I shouldn't have had that second great one, later, and the city comes into view. UPenn is like its own little world within the city limits. With unique architecture, a park, and courtyards that divide the campus. It's all colorful, gables and stone. The Famous LOVE Statue. Following the directions to the visitor center, we park. Now the real adventure begins.

I'll save you the ten cent tour we were taken on, suffice to say the campus is huge, and I'm stoked to be becoming a part of the UPenn family. Kaycee was fairly quiet but chatted it up with a few people in the tour group. We break by lunchtime, which is just in time to check-in at The Penn Inn, the place we're staying for the next two days.

The room is a king and done up in blues and reds the college's colors. "It's nice." I say, sitting on the bed.

"Yeah, sure," Kaycee says, sounding distant.

"Hey, what's up?"

"Nothing, I'm hungry is all. Wanna check out the dining room I saw on our way up?"

"We can." I know something is up she just is being too evasive. I don't want to fight with her, though. I let it go. For now, maybe she is just getting hangry.

The restaurant at the Inn is a bit... *much*, we opt to find something more casual.

A little looking and we find, *Baby Blues BBQ*. It's casual style and food? *Reasonable*, though, I can tell that some of the prices make her squirm. I reach across the booth. "Hey? Why are you on edge? We're away from all the humorless asshats and supposed to be enjoying ourselves."

"I- it's just..." She looks at her hands in her lap. "I'm seeing what you have to look forward to, and I can' t help but think..."

"Think what? Kayce talk to me." I pull her across the booth to sit beside me.

"How do I fit into all this? I mean, how am I supposed to keep with you if you're gone?"

I hadn't thought about it. About us not being together after the summer. She wasn't going to UPenn, I was. Was I leaving her behind? Could I now? "We'll figure it out."

"Will we? I mean, am I just supposed to

drive out on weekends, hang out, then go home. Work my menial job and pine for four years and hope you don't meet someone you like better?"

"That's not how this is gonna work."

"Yeah? You sure? I mean, I saw how these girls look at you. I can't compete with them. I will never be able to."

"There's no contest. You have me. they don't," I try to assure her. "C'mon, let's just have a bit of fun. Unwind a little; I think we both deserve it."

"You're talking about going to that party, Pat the tour guide handed out the flyer for?"

"Why not?"

"You don't *do* parties. You study." She reminds me.

"Well, maybe the new independent me wants to try it on for size."

"Alright." She smiles, leaning into me as the food comes. She takes a fry and pops it into her mouth. "At least the food's good."

***

The party is at a private residence just three blocks south of the Ben Franklin bench. Figuring there will be alcohol Kaycee and I Uber it. I wish it was warmer because the campus is beautiful, even at night. Arches and gardens that, even in the winter, sleep foretell the blooms to come. Arriving, the place seems quiet until the door opens, and the sound system hits us.

"Welcome prospects!" The guy at the door shouts. "Five bucks gets you a cup then it's all you can consume."

I hand the guy a ten.

"Nice. You and the pretty one, here you are, there's a marker to put your name on the cup. *Don't* lose your cup." He hands us lidded screw-top cups with straws. "Enjoy!"

"This is gonna be interesting." I snicker as we head inside.

"We'll see." Kaycee smirks, holding on to me and her cup.

CHAPTER 18

KAYCEE

Ouch! My head is killing me. Where the hell am I? My eyes adjust to the low lighting of the room. The curtains are drawn, but light still filters through the mini-blinds. I feel heavy. I try to move, but I'm pinned. "Cal?" I whisper. Trying to push him off. Only the person rolling into me has got a pair of tits that rival Dolly Parton. *What the fuck?* I go to wiggle away and am hugged by a guy that smells like money and broken dreams. I drag my naked body up the head of the bed, and as my eyes adjust, I finally see Cal. He's got two blondes on him as he's out on the floor.

I hold my head, trying to piece together what happened. I remember drinks, pizza. Dancing. Then some people passing around a couple of joints. Flashes of what happened start to come to me. Cal and I finding a room. *This room*, then more people. Those big tits in my face, mouths on me. My mouth on others. Cal and this passed out guy, going at me, *together*.

My body aches as I search for my clothes. I can't even look at him. I get out of there. I need to get out of here. I need a pharmacy.

Plan B in the bag I go back to the Inn, by the time I get there, Cal is back.

"Hey." He grabs me, hugging me. "I don't know what happened. Last night-"

"I took care of myself," I say, being smothered by him. "Can we not talk about it?"

"Are you alright?"

"Yeah. I need a shower, though."

"Of course."

"Join me?" I ask as I'm taking off my blouse. I just need to erase what happened. I need for him to not look at me and see what I think he saw. A wanton whore that couldn't be satisfied by one man, so I took on the whole room.

"Are you sure?" He eyes me, curiously.

I toss my bra at him. "Come and get it."

He starts stripping off his clothes, and we hit the shower in a flurry of kisses. His hard cock presses into my belly.

"I need to grab a condom." He pulls away, but I pull him back.

"I have another dose of Plan B. Just fuck me. Consider it your birthday present." I step into the warmth of the shower. He joins me and pinning me to the wall, lifts me. We kiss as he preps me with his wandering fingers. I put a foot up on the side of the shower stall giving him ample access. His cock slips up and down my tender slit. He presses in then pulls back, getting just his tip wet. "Cal, c'mon." I beg as he teases me.

"You want *this*? Want *me*? *Just* me?" He presses into me slowly, opening me up little by little.

"*Yes.* God in heaven, *yes.*" The feeling of him raw inside me is intense. The resistance, pressure, *friction.* I've never gone bareback.

Now, I think we're gonna have to look into some kind of birth control because I don't think I want to go back to condoms. I rise and fall against him, coming quickly. Once I come, he stops and washes me down. It's tender and feels *so* good. He rubs every inch of flesh. Then I do the same for him, of course, I can't keep my mouth to myself and what started as a rub down, turns to a blown load. Picking me up, he takes me to bed, where we forego the rest of the day, to fuck and indulge in room service.

CHAPTER 19

CALVIN

So much for seminars and tours. I spent my birthday eve balls deep in warm wet pussy. Kaycee indulged me. *Repeatedly.* This morning is no exception. I open my eyes to her sucking my cock before climbing on to me. She bounces on me, and I lay back, enjoying the visual. Her little tits popping up and down as she grabs one with her hand. The other hand is between us. She grasps my sac while I rub her sensitive clit. The headboard slams against the wall, and the neighbors bang. Kaycee's answer?

"Oh! Calvin! Fuck me, baby! Harder! Faster! That's it, baby, you know how I need it!" As she smashes her little body against me *and* the headboard.

"They're gonna send someone up." I grit out, through heavy pants.

"We're checking out anyhow. May as well make it memorable.- Oh! Calvin!" She exaggerates, but it does it for me, and I shoot deep into her.

We clean up and grabbing a bag full of McGriddles, and hash browns are on the road by nine-thirty. Kaycee sleeps most of the way as I drive us home. It's fine as frankly she's earned it. When we get to the house, there are balloons outside, and as I grab the bags, Tracie greets us at the door.

"Happy Birthday, Calvin!" She's got a cake with my name on it and the numbers one and eight.

I raise an eyebrow.

"Make a wish and blow out the candles. It's homemade. Chocolate marble. I hope that's' okay?"

I smile, blowing out the candles. "Thank you." I haven't had a real birthday, with a cake in years. My mother felt it was an unnecessary indulgence.

"C'mon. I've been baking a pork shoulder since yesterday. Pulled it a few hours ago, it should be perfect for sandwiches now. Also made baked mac and cheese plus corn pudding."

"A real feast, mom." Kaycee smiles as we head inside. There are more balloons, streamers, and a banner that says *Happy Birthday!*

This may not be my actual family, but they sure treat me like their own. What about my fucked people? I haven't heard one peep since I left.

I go to fix a plate when my phone rings. Excusing myself, I answer.

"Hello?"

"Cal! Happy Birthday buddy!"

"Uncle Douglas?"

"Yeah, long time no talk. Did you get my gift?"

"Um- you sent a gift?"

"You not checking your email? Boy, you got mail!"

I look at my email folder. I had an alert from PayPal. " Twenty-Five hundred bucks?" I say, shocked.

"I talked to your father. He told me what happened."

"I'm sorry I've let everyone down."

"What? No. Cal, fuck them. You need to follow your bliss. You and that girl, if she's your bliss, then you're one lucky bastard. You love her?"

"I think so." I watch her as she sets up two plates, smiling to me as our eyes connect. "Yeah."

"You hold on to her then. No matter what. Don't wind up like your Uncle Douglas, fifty and alone with just your money. It's not everything. If you got love, you're the richest man on the planet. But if you need anything you call. Got me?"

"I got you, Uncle Douglas. Thank you."

"Eh, No worries. Now I got eighteen holes waiting for me. I'll talk to you soon. Love ya, kid."

"Yeah? Love you too." I hang up the phone as Kaycee comes up to me with piled-up plates. "Thanks."

"Oh, you think this is for you?" She pulls the plate from me, playfully. "I need the carbs."

"Shut it, or I'll give you something to shut it with." I take the plate. It smells wonderful.

"Who was that?" She inquires.

"Uncle Douglas, he sent me some cash

for the birthday. Looks like I got what I need for the registration of the Santa Fe."

"Yeah? Cool."

"Oh, Calvin?" Tracie calls over.

"Yes?" I say, taking a seat at the dining table.

"A guy from Version Wireless called me about you. I didn't know you applied for a job."

"I can't just live here free." I answer. "Besides, school is gonna be expensive, especially living off-campus."

Kaycee looks at me, confused. "Why won't you be in the dorms?"

"I don't think they'll approve of my living situation."

Grandpa Compton chuckles. The old man knows where my head is at even if the girls don't. "I think he's askin' you a big question, Seabee."

"Huh?" Her eyes go wide, "What? I don't get it."

"If I learned anything from this weekend, it's that I am going to be having to adjust to a lot when I leave. What I don't want to adjust to is time away from you." I push one of her unruly curls behind her ear.

"That's not gonna happen. What's out there for her?" Tracie asks, getting it now.

"What's here?" I say in rebuttal. "She's got management experience, like you, there's a community tech school literally down the road from UPenn, there's opportunity. There's a way out of here."

"Wait, are you asking me to leave with you?"

"Now, you've got it." I smile, patting her on the head; she tries to bite my hand. "Come to UPenn, *be with me.*"

She looks at her mom and Grandpa. Grandpa is nodding yes, Tracie looks terrified. "Mom?"

"Baby, you're an adult, and as much as I wanna keep you here, here, you drown."

"Seabee, it's time to sail away."

"But what about you and mom?"

"Oh, I think we'll manage. I'm going to get that prosthetic, and it'll all be good. You just watch." Grandpa Compton insists.

"What do I do?" She says, unsure.

"*You* apply to the Community College of Philadelphia, and *we* start looking for a place asap."

"Are we really gonna do this?"

"Yeah. We are." I smile, and she wraps her arms around me.

Kissing me, she whispers. "I love you."

CHAPTER 20

KAYCEE

I'm so in love! What's better than that? We're going to start a new life together, in Pennsylvania. Away from all the closed-minded and small people of Cradle Bay. Sure it'll be an adjustment, and we've promised no more parties, but new can be good.

It's been a couple of weeks since all of that crazy, and I'm going to find and shoot that groundhog. He *lied*. Said an early spring, ha! Sub-arctic temperatures and snow! In MARCH! I've been freezing Cal out the last few days as it's that time, and I'm just not ready to explore *that* kind of intimacy. I'm sure he's not the squeamish type, but after my experience with Heath, I'm inclined to say nay. It's light this month, but I'm stressing, so it's expected. Cal brought up Prom *again*. He still wants to go. It's gonna be an adjustment, as he no longer has unlimited funds, but he says he doesn't care. He won't miss out on the milestones, especially now that it's me and him till the wheels fall off.

Things have started to quiet down at school, *finally*. They stopped posting the video. Mostly because there was an incident with an Assistant Teacher and one of the girls on the swim team. *Scandalous,* I know! I mean, I shouldn't be reveling in someone else's misery, but I'm just glad the spotlight is off us finally.

Cal still hasn't talked to his family. They haven't even tried to reach out. Not a call, or email, text. *Nothing.* They did, however, cut off his cellphone. Fortunately, he got the job at Verison, so service discount! Jokes on them. Cal is doing *so* good. Enjoying his freedom, though he's way too easy to order around. I guess years being under the thumb of an abusive mom can do that. We, mom, and me are trying to be mindful of his little ticks. The need to keep the peace, always put things away. Keep things in an orderly way. Grandpa loves it. He's alphabetized our bookshelves, our DVDs and Blue-rays, CDs. It has been an adjustment and way insightful. I know what I'm in for living with him, at least.

Spotless home and orgasms before bed every night. I call it a good deal. I'm outside waiting on Cal. We're headed out to the Macy's. He wants to look into a new suit and a dress for me. He's been hanging on to the birthday money from Uncle Douglas and has decided it's our Prom stash.

He comes out and looks a little scruffy. I hadn't noticed, but he's not shaved in a few days. I stop him. Grabbing the strawberry blonde whiskers, he's got started. "Why, if you're blonde, are your whiskers red?"

"I don't know." He smiles down at me.

"You trying a new look or run out of blades?"

"New look, thinking about a goatee."

"Could be sexy, just don't go Duck Dynasty on me." I kiss him as he unlocks the Santa Fe. Since he got this, I've let mom have the van back. Why drive two cars, especially when his has heated seats? You know what I'm saying?

"How did we do that?" Cal asks me astonished as we leave Macy's with everything we need and still have enough for lunch with plenty of change.

"It's called a *sale;* you're not *Mister Moneybags* anymore, so we had to be creative. I just know how to squeeze a penny till it farts is all."

I got a sweet as sin royal blue gown. It's got this crocheted halter top and sides that show just enough skin, and a split front to let me actually walk. Paired up with strappy glittery silver heels and a pair of teardrop earrings, and I'm complete. We found him a slim fit Perry Ellis tux that made me just want to strip him, right there in the dressing room. I, of course, being so little, easily climbed under the door and got my mouthful, for which he has promised to reciprocate as soon as I let him back into the panty zone.

Having been my friend for years, he knows how to take care of me during this week. Heating pads, chocolate ice cream, and all the greasy food I can get. It's off to the food court for some Panda Express and Sbarro Pizza.

"I'm gonna hit the bathroom; you get us

a spot to sit?" I say, kissing him on the cheek.

"I got it." He grins at me as his phone rings.

I just keep going, got things to take care of in the girly bit department.

CHAPTER 21

CALVIN

Prom will be a success. Thank God for one decent person in my family. I called in a couple favors with my Uncle Douglas, and everything is set. See, he owns a limo service, among other things, in New York, so he's hooking us up with a white stretch, stocked with snacks and one bottle of good champagne. So long as we promise to not drink it until after prom. He's sending down his stylist to take care of Kaycee and me for the big day, and he gave me an advance on a little something extra. *What*? I got her something from James Allen. An exquisite half-carat emerald cut diamond with side set sapphire stones to match her eyes. I've decided that if we're gonna do this, we may as well do it all the way. I'll be talking to Grandpa Compton this week while she's at work. I feel it only fitting to ask him and Tracie both before I just go off and do it. I want them on board. We're going to need somebody at the wedding after all.

"Hey? Where are you?" Kayce asks me as I've gone into my head, thinking about how

I'm going to pop the question. Do I put it in her champagne? In a slice of her favorite cheesecake? You know like they do in the movies? Probably not, my luck she'd swallow it, and we'd spend Prom night in the ER while they pumped her stomach. Best to just do the old fashioned knee drop. I'm having blue roses delivered to her all week, One per class by a freshman from the Science club. They took white roses and naturally dyed them just for us.

"I'm here. I was just imagining you in that dress."

"You should see what I'm planning to wear *under it*." She teases me, her hand on my thigh.

"Show me later?"

"Nuh-uh. You have to wait till Prom night." Deflecting my kiss, she pops a fried shrimp into her mouth. "Hmm, so good."

"You are a terrible tease."

"Oh? Am *I*." She unzips my pants, and I drop a napkin in my lap. She grasps me, stroking me till I'm good and hard.

I look around, people are going about their business, and here I am getting a handjob. Christ, she's good at this. "You need to finish eating."

"Why? You got somewhere to be?"

"No, but you do, and I plan to pound you for at least twenty minutes before you have to go to work."

She looks at me with narrowing eyes. "It may still be a little funky down there."

"We'll stop for a towel set." I insist with a groan as she stops.

"Okay." She sips her Coke, with a happy little dance in her seat.

I parked in the underground garage, we get to the truck, and she's climbed straight into the back. I find a spot where there aren't many cars and repark.

She's stripped from the waist down and put the towels we bought under her. I join her in the back and undo my pants. "You are cool with this, right?"

She nods. "I knew we were gonna break this thing in *eventually*."

"Oh, you did? Did you?" I laugh, pulling her down toward my cock. I go to enter her, but she's kind of dry. I contemplate spitting on my junk, then decide that is not what you do with a woman you want to marry. I top her, kissing her. I'll get those juices flowing the *right way*. I get my cock, so it's rubbing her clit as I move up and down on her. She moans. There we go. Lifting her shirt, I lick and suck her pert little nipples. I love how dark pink they seem to be lately. Like she's blushing, my cock slips down and in between her folds. I hit her juicy center. In and over the ridge, I start at her. Slow at first as she's still not quite there. I pull out, then dip back in, having her ass overhead, I keep doing this till she's so wet I can hear every inch of me as it sinks into her. Grabbing her ass, I start to pound her. Harder, she's pushing against my thrusts with her hands on the window.

"Oh! Cal." She pants, "That's it. Fuck me, Harder." She's been getting more vocal. More open about what she likes, how she wants me to fuck her. She likes any position where we can keep eye contact; it makes her come like a cat for the nip. I take her hands, holding them up above her head as I work her.

"I'm gonna come." I warn, like a good little pixie, she hops back and sucks my cock into her mouth to finish me off. This has been our go-to since UPenn. No more condoms. I know it's risky, but would a baby be so bad?

CHAPTER 22

KAYCEE

Work sucks tonight. All that sex this afternoon, brought my period back, and Rosie, one of my employees only had pads. So I have been walking around in a practical diaper all night. In these pants, it's hard to hide too. It's been busy. So much so that I had to come out and assist. I rarely have to do orders anymore, but when I do, I show them how it's *done,* that's for sure. Since Heath and I stopped seeing each other, he and his cronies don't come round like they used to. At least they *weren't*. But with March comes the return of baseball season. I'm not the type to bitch, but I hate that he knows me so well.

"Hey, McLane, you still trying to move on up?" Heath comes in, and I grit my teeth.

"This is my workplace; don't make me throw you out. Order something, or please leave." I say as kind and as stern as I can.

"I want a double bacon egg and cheese on a croissant, hash browns, and a mocha coffee coolatta."

"Anything else?"

"How about another shot?"
"Yeah? I don't think so."
"C'mon, don't you miss me at all?"

I look up at the ceiling. "Umm, let me think. No. Not at all."

"Bull shit."

"Look, Heath, we had a good time, but let's call it for what it was. Just that. You got to explore your more *experimental* side, and I got to come on occasion without having to do it myself. I didn't love you. You sure as fuck didn't love me. So let's just call a spade a spade. No hard feelings. *Okay*?"

"*Yeah... Okay.*"

I give him his order, and he takes it out. Thank God! I don't think I could have dealt with him sticking around.

****

It's just after eleven-forty, and it's dead. I look around outside. No cars. "Hey, Rosie? Why don't you take off? I'll close up."

"You sure?"

"Yeah, Tom will be here in like twenty minutes to start tomorrow's batches, so I should be fine."

"Okay, I'll just use my keys."

"Sounds good. Have a good night." I say, taking pots into the back to wash.

I'm about to turn on the water when I hear her voice.

"You got a visitor!"
"What kind?"
"The tall and sexy kind!"

I smile, Cal is early. "Send him back!"

I start doing the dishes when I catch his shadow. Hands slip up my uniform top, cupping my breasts as lips connect with my neck.

"We can't, Cal. I need to finish this." I roll my head to the side. He leans into me, and I realize that the cock pressing into me, is *way* lower than it should be. I spin around and see it's Heath. "What the fuck?" I hiss. He's got one of the bagel knives.

"You and me, we gonna play a game."

"Fuck all we are." I swallow as he grabs me. The knife against my side.

"You're gonna suck my cock, or I'm gonna cut that pretty little face of yours." He's got my hair, pushing me to the wet floor.

I try to resist, but he nicks my cheek, "Oh! Okay." I sputter tears in my eyes. He whips out his dick and slaps me in the face with it.

"You know how I like it, and if you even think of biting me- I will do more than just a paper cut."

I do as he demands, making sure to do it like he likes, so he starts to get into it. He's got me by the head, the knife sorta to the side. I'm looking for a way to get away. I see a coffee pot that I had set aside, it's empty, but it'll have to do. I look up; he's closed his eyes. Here's my chance. I grab the pot and smash it against him. He howls as I scramble, slipping along the floor. I run to the front of the shop. He catches up to me by hopping the counter. Grabbing me, he wrestles me to the floor. I scream. Slashing his face with my keys.

"Bitch!" He growls. His bloodied face dripping on to me. "Now, you're *really* gonna scream, and ain't nobody round to hear it." He rips my pants down. I kick and scream again. It's no use he's got me pinned. "Ugh, you're raggin', again? Christ, do you ever *not* bleed?" He flips me over, smacking my ass. "Guess we'll improvise."

I cry out as he spreads me open and spits into me. "I always wanted a piece of ass from you." He grunts, impaling me. My face is covered in tears as I try to go somewhere else in my head. Anywhere but here. *Please, God, somebody, stop him...*

***

Opening my eyes, I'm disorientated. I'm moving. I'm strapped down as someone flashes a bright light in my eyes.

"Kaycee, can you hear me?" A woman asks. I freak- screaming, trying to get up.

"Calm down, sweetie. I'm a nurse at the Cradle Bay emergency room. You were attacked, but you are safe now."

"Let me up!" I scream. "Please!" I whimper, falling apart.

"We're gonna transfer you to another bed; then we need to do a rape kit. Okay?"

"No, don't fucking touch me!"

"Kayce!" I hear Cal calling my name.

My cries become sobs. "Please don't let him back here. I- he can't know."

"He's the one that brought you in."

"No! No, no, no..."

CHAPTER 23

CALVIN

"So, you heard the screaming, and then what?" The officer asks me for the fifth time to tell my side of the story. See, I couldn't stop what happened. I was too late for that.

"I told you I saw him on her, and when I couldn't get the door opened, I did the- the only thing I could think of."

"And that's when you drove through the front window, hitting the victim?"

"Victim my ass. That piece of shit had just raped my girlfriend. Go look at her; she's cut up and bleeding from every hole he could violate!" I growl.

"Take it easy, son." The officer insists. "I am just trying to get a clear picture of what happened."

"I arrived to pick Kaycee up from closing, Saw her, *and* him, heard her screaming. Busted into the place, knocking and pinning Heath Cramer to the counter. I didn't kill him, so let me be. Go arrest him for assault."

"You need to stick around. We may have more questions."

"Whatever. I'm going to see my girl." I

push by the rolly polly officer and head back to the room where they moved Kaycee after finally doing their checkups.

Walking in, she's sitting up, her hands in her lap just staring at the blankets covering her. "Hey?" I whisper.

She bites her lip. "I'm sorry." She sniffles. "I'm so sorry."

"For what, this wasn't your fault."

"I'm pregnant." She blurts out softly.

"Wait- *what*?" I'm standing at the side of the bed. I couldn't have heard her right.

"About five and a half weeks, they think."

"But- you have your period."

"They say that sometimes happens, especially in younger girls. I'm sorry. I'll get rid of it if that's what you want." She cries, holding her stomach.

"I'd never ask that of you." I pull her into me, and she flinches. "We'll figure it out."

"Baby?" I hear Tracie coming.

"Please, we can't tell her. Not yet. *Okay?*"

I nod, not letting her go.

The curtain pulls, and there is Tracie *and* Grandpa Compton.

"Heard you put that shit bag in the hospital. Good for you." Grandpa Compton gruffs. Wheeling to us, he touches her foot. "You're gonna be okay."

Kaycee nods. Holding on to me. "Nothing that won't heal." She says softly. "Nothing that won't heal."

***

They keep Kaycee overnight for

observation. I refuse to leave her side. She sleeps, a lot and wakes with a start a few times. I have to stroke her hair until she falls asleep again.

I hear from one of the other nurses that Heath was also here. Handcuffed to his bed, in a guarded room. It's a good fucking thing because if I could get to him- I'd fucking kill him. I shattered his leg from the knee down. Glad to hear it. Dunkin' has closed its doors seeing as it's got a gaping hole through the front of the shop. What else was I supposed to do? Let him cut her throat?

She's got stitches in her cheek, but other than that, her injuries are less *visible*. How she's going to cope with the rape remains to be seen.

As we are getting her ready to leave the hospital, there's a knock on the door. I like how they knock, like for permission, but then just come in anyhow.

"Hi there." A tall, slender woman enters. "Are you Kaycee?"

Kaycee nods, pulling on her sneakers. "Yup. What can I do for you?"

"I'm Bonnie, Mercer. I work for the local chapter of SARC, here in Delaware."

"SARC? What's that." I ask.

"It's the rape crisis center," Kaycee answers flatly. "One of you came in last night to see me, tossed a card at me."

"Yes, that was Wendy. She is sorry for her abruptness and didn't mean to upset you."

"I wasn't ready to be talking to anyone. I'd just come to after being brutalized."

"Yes, and I understand. I'm sorry, but we *are* here to help. In any way, you may need."

Kaycee stands up with a hard sigh. "Honestly? I just want to put this as far behind me as I can. Thank you, though."

"Well, I have a packet here, would you humor me in taking it at least?"

"Sure." She answers with an eye roll.

Bonnie hands it to me as Kaycee goes into the bathroom, dragging the IV pole with her. "If she needs anything, we're just a phone call away. Same goes for you."

"But I wasn't-"

"No, but you may find your whole world is about to change."

"Thank you, Bonnie."

She nods and takes her leave, just as the nurse returns with the wheelchair so we can blow this joint.

CHAPTER 24

KAYCEE

I'm gonna lose my shit. All I do now is sleep or cry when no one looks. I'm trying desperately to not shrink away from the touch of others.

I'm just getting off the phone when Cal comes in to check on me. He's been ditching lunch to come home to bring me my guilty pleasures. Cheesesteaks from *The Cheese Steak factory* with extra bacon, provolone, peppers, and mushrooms. He also gets a bucket of cheese fries and Iced Tea to wash it all down. I don't think I could love him more right now.

"Hey, I got grub, who was that?" He asks curiously. I hadn't been taking calls, so seeing me on the phone is odd for him.

"That?" I say, watching as he dumps out the food. "My store manager Rudy. He said that I could have all the time off I need. That they were gonna pay me for it too. Guess they're afraid I'm gonna sue or some shit. I'd never do that. What happened wasn't *their* fault. He also said that if I wanted to transfer to another shop, he would understand. *That*

I will probably do." I touch my face. I'm gonna have a scar on my cheek from where Heath cut me. He saw to it.

"That's probably best. Detective Rice had me pulled from second period."

I raise a brow.

"Wanted to let me know that no charges were being brought against me for my vandalism or shit faces' injury."

My boyfriend, in my defense, saw to ending my attacker's baseball career with the front bumper of the Santa Fe. "Good. I'm glad he's still in the hospital. I wish he'd been killed. Though jail is probably gonna do him wonders. A pretty boy like him, I'm sure he'll get to do plenty of butt stuff." I stuff the sandwich into my mouth with a half-grin.

"That's a healthy way to look at it." Cal chuckles. "I think that's the first smile I've seen since we got you home."

I instantly frown. "I'm sorry. I know that this is not easy for you." I put down the tasty num, nums. "Sleeping next to someone that won't let you touch her."

"I spent fourteen years *not* touching you like that. I think I can hold out."

"You shouldn't have to, though. I'd understand if you need to seek it elsewhere."

Cal looks at me like I've just shot him in the chest. "Kayce, none of that matters. All that matters is that you are gonna be okay. That you're here, that you don't shut me out completely."

I nod. My sleep has been broken except when he's in bed with me. It's the only time I feel safe. "Will you lay down with me? Just till I fall asleep?"

"Of course," Cal answers sweetly. We eat, and then he climbs into bed with me. Holding me and stroking my hair until the world falls away and darkness takes hold.

***

I wake up covered in sweat and trembling. I've had another nightmarish rehash of what happened. Every time it happens, it's more vivid. The sounds of him grunting against me. His breath on my back. The pain in my body as he tore me up. It's almost three. Cal won't be home until after nine. He's got work up at the Verizon store. I'm edgy. I need to do *something*. Heading down the hall, I see mom and grandpa watching tv. I look around desperately for an escape. Seeing the car keys, I grab them, my shoes, and am out the door. I'm not sure where I'm going until I'm here. The local WYMCA, which according to the cards from Bonnie and Wendy, also happens to be the local chapter of SARC's location.

I park and go inside. Looking around, I see the signs that point in the right direction. I follow, then walk into the SARC waiting area. There are women buzzing around like little worker bees. I hesitate and turn ready to tuck tail when I hear my name.

"Kaycee?"

I look back, seeing Miss Warner, Cal's Physics teacher. "Christ," I whisper, looking at myself. Ratty clothes, hair all jacked up. No makeup. I look like a bag lady. "Hi, um I was- just."

"It's okay." She puts out her hand to me. "You want a bottle of water, soda? Maybe a cup of hot tea?" Her voice is gentle. *Kind.* I need a little kindness right now. I let her lead me past the front desk.

"A coke? You work here too?" I ask, confused.

"I volunteer as a peer group leader."

"Peer?"

She smiles shortly. "I'm an abuse survivor. So I have a bit of insight, I suppose. I connect with the others here in ways some of the other SARA's don't."

I nod. Taking the cold Coke. "I don't even know why I'm here."

"Because you need to be. We're here for you. If you need to talk, one on one, groups, whatever you need."

"Groups?" I ask, unsure.

"Yes, you'd be surprised how many young people are affected by some kind of sexual trauma every day, even in a town as small as Cradle Bay. My open talk group has space. If you'd like to sit in."

I think I'd like that." I smile.

CHAPTER 25

CALVIN

A week until prom. I told Kaycee we didn't have to go, but she's insisted that it's important. That it's part of getting back to *normal*. She's started going over to the WYMCA three days a week. She attends a couple of groups and is seeing someone on an individual basis. I'm thankful she's talking to someone, even if that person isn't me. We've started looking at apartments online for after graduation. Totally her doing. I am not trying to pressure her in any way. She's slowly getting back to being the smiling, joking girl I've known all my life. Due mostly in part to Heath's pleading no contest to the rape and assault. They had him dead to rights with DNA, and the video cameras in the shop. There was no sense in a drawn-out trial. He's in county lockup pending his sentence, confined to a wheelchair because they won't let him have crutches.

I'm sitting in the living room with Tracie and grandpa Compton when a Zale's commercial comes on. I hadn't altered my plans to propose. It has just been in the back of my head, with the more pressing matters at hand.

I clear my throat gaining their attention. Kayce is at her meeting, so it's just the three of us. "Well, guess I'm on it now." I chuckle.

"You got something to say, boy?"

"Yeah, actually, I do. I stand up, as to be taken seriously. "As you know, Kayce and I are going to be leaving in just a couple of months."

Nods from them, an eyebrow raise from Tracie.

"Well, I've thought about this, and I want to ask your permission for us to get married."

Crickets.

"Look—I'm not going into this lightly. I know it's gonna be hard. But we are gonna be living together. If we're married we can get Student subsidy, and other help as well."

"You don't have any idea what marriage would be like. You can't just walk away from marriage." Tracie says bitterly.

"Trace, stop. Don't project what happened with you and that bum on to these two."

She goes to speak, but he silences her. "You wanna marry? Now?"

"I'm thinking that depends on Kaycee; I want to at least get engaged. That makes us look better to potential landlords, and well, I've already bought the ring."

CHAPTER 26

KAYCEE

"I just can't shake it. This feeling that if I'd just been *smarter*."

"Kaycee, what happened wasn't your fault. You didn't do *anything* wrong." Miss Warner says to me as we sit in the Open talk group.

"I know you say that, but if I'd have followed procedure that night, not let Rosie leave early..."

"Are you going to go back on that loop?" Micha is a fourteen-year-old boy who was raped by his uncle for six years before he finally spoke up, starts. "We are the ones who were *hurt*. Taken advantage of, *terrorized*. We have to stop giving the predators a pass based on our own behaviors." He looks at me intently. "I was told every time he violated me that if I wasn't so damn cute, he wouldn't have had to do it. Look at me." Half his face is cut up and scared. He put his head through a mirror when he was twelve, in hopes it would deter his rapist. He was raped again while in the hospital, which was when they caught the bastard, finally.

"I'm sorry, Micha," I whisper.

"Don't apologize to me. *Apologize* to you. C'mon, Kaycee, you need to forgive yourself for that night and thank that boyfriend for putting a car through the fucker."

I chuckle. Micha was passionate. He was an advocate. He was a formidable ally.

"There ya go. If I was you, I'd go home and make sweet, sweet love to that sexy boy, and remember what it is like to be with a person who loves you, *for real.*"

"We have Prom coming. He's gone all out." I say with genuine cheer. "I never thought I'd be excited to go to a school function, but since the *incident*, things have been better for us at school. They named Cal, Valedictorian. He's gonna have to give a speech and everything." I say my hands in my lap.

"There you go." Miss Warner chirps. "Looking forward is good. Let's break it there for the day. There are refreshments provided by Marci's bakery this week."

We separate, and Micha comes over to me and hugs me. I settle into him. His hugs are good. Warm. *Safe.* He pulls back, and we walk over to the baked goodies. Miss Warner catches me as I got to sit.

"Hey? You got a minute?"

"Sure." I look back at Micha, and he waves at me to go stuffing a tartlet in his mouth.

"Not that it's my business, but do you plan to tell the group?"

"Tell them what?" I say, as my eyes follow hers to my hand on the small bump I'm forming. I've been wearing big shirts and a lot of yoga pants lately, but the instinct to protect the growing life in me seems stronger than I realize. "I—how did you?"

"I caught you in silhouette against the backlight. Noticed the pooch. We're trained to spot this sorta thing; sometimes girls come in and don't' understand what's happening. Was it?"

"Oh, no, Cal. It was before. I'm ten weeks. I think."

"You *think*? Haven't you been to an OBGYN?"

I shake my head.

"Would you like to?"

"I dunno. I mean, what can they tell me other than yup, bun in the oven?"

"Oh, honey. C'mon, we'll go now."

"*Now*, but don't I like—need an appointment?"

"I'm assuming you don't plan to tell Tracie yet?"

I nod vehemently.

"Planned Parenthood in Wilmington is just fifteen minutes up the road. They have later hours today. If we go now, we can get in."

"Oh—Okay." I stutter and let Miss Warner lead me outside. "Do you want me to drive, or do you feel more comfortable doing it?"

"I—I guess we can go in your car."

She nods. "You should probably call me April, after all, it's not like we're at the school anymore." She says, leading me to her Tahoe.

Fifteen minutes and I'm in the front

offices of my first Planned Parenthood. A stack of paperwork in front of me. Miss Warn—April helps me fill out the financial stuff, and by six-fifteen, I'm on a cold metal table with some lady all up in my hoo-ha!

"Okay, you're gonna feel a little pressure; it's totally normal."

April holds my hand, and the exam is conducted. I'm lying there, and this doctor turns a monitor to me. "It would seem you're approximately thirteen weeks along. According to the date of your last actual period in January." She goes on. "Things look good. See this?" She points to the monitor. "See that? That's *your* baby."

My eyes pop, seeing the bulbous head and little body. "That head is HUGE! Is that normal?"

The doctor laughs. "Completely. Would you like to hear its heartbeat?"

I squeeze April's hand. "*Please.*"

She turns on the sound, and an echoing sound like hummingbirds wings fills the room. "It's so fast."

"Healthy?" April asks.

"So far, so good. Though I would stress starting a prenatal vitamin. How is your morning sickness?"

"I haven't really had any. Is that bad?" I ask, concerned.

"No, just makes you a lucky momma to be." She hits print on the screen and after getting me situated, hands me a copy of what we had seen. "Baby's first selfie." She smiles.

"We can give you your first month of vitamins. You can get more over the counter, or if you'd rather pick them up when you come back in, that's fine too."

"Back?"

"There is a continuation of care here, Kaycee. We will help monitor your journey through this pregnancy."

"What if I move away? I'm supposed to go to Pennsylvania with the father." I touch my belly.

"We can transfer your records to any Planned Parenthood in the country. You just let us know when and where."

"Thank you."

"No problem. Do you have any questions?"

"Not really. I mean, what is there to know? I'm due in early October; I need to eat well, get plenty of fluids, and sleep. Keep stress low and take the vitamins."

"There's more to it, but I think you'll be okay for now. We have a booklet you can take home or online info if you please."

"Thank you."

"You are welcome. See you back here in say two weeks?"

"I have exams."

"Right, *high school*." The doctor says shortly. "How's May Sixth? And again on the twentieth?"

"Sounds like a plan."

CHAPTER 27

CALVIN

The house is in upheaval. My Uncle Douglas wasn't kidding when he said he'd take care of us. A salon bus appeared last night, and that was the last I saw of my soon to be fiancée. They even took Tracie and gave her a new do' and mani-pedi for the occasion.

I got a fresh clip, making my ponytail far less ratty. My goatee is now perfectly edged as they waxed my face! That shit hurt! But I do have to say it looks better, and my cheeks are smoother than my ass! I may have to keep up with the waxing if these are *typical* results.

It's an hour till we have to arrive when I hear the front door open.

"Cal?" It's my uncle.

I come out, surprised to see him. "What are you doing?" He cuts me silent showing me the ring. Tracie gasps her hand to her heart. "You alright?" The box claps close as it's put it to my hand.

"You must be Tracie McLane. Kaycee's mother." He smiles his debonair smile and takes her hand gently. "I see where she gets her beauty from."

"T-thank you." Tracie blushes.

"Oh, bother." I snicker. *"Really?"*

"Shush boy. Go get done; you have pictures in twenty."

"Pictures?"

"Of course, I hired a photographer. They scouted out a beautiful spot up the way, a covered bridge, with climbing ivy and honeysuckle in bloom."

"Uh-huh." I shake my head and go to finish up. Heading outside, I wait, with the rest of her bouquet of roses. Yup, I had those freshmen for hire, and they did a wonderful job. She comes out, and I lose my breath. The dress looks phenomenal on her, and her hair is curly! Half swept up, off her face, as a sapphire tiara crowns her head. The earrings sparkle, and her makeup is low key, pretty, except for her lips; they are ruby red and sparkling.

Her eyes light up, seeing me, and that bottom lip disappears into her mouth. It seems like me; she likes what she sees. I go to her with the flowers, and she kisses my cheek.

"You look so handsome."

"Thank you, gorgeous."

We get into the limo and start our ride toward the covered bridge. It's a really nice spot, and I'm surprised more people don't use it for pictures.

Getting out first, I help Kaycee. She's got a little clutch bag with her. It's weird because she doesn't usually carry a purse.

"I have a gift for you." She sparkles.

"Yeah, okay." I can't stop smiling like a fool. I have the ring. I plan to pop the question before we go into the prom.

We pose a few times, and the photographer talks us through how to move, we take a short break for him to change his lens, and that's when she lays her gift on me.

Opening her clutch, she pulls out a little envelope. "Here."

I crook a curious brow. Opening it, I'm faced with the first picture of our baby, and it brings me to my knees.

"Oh, my God! Are you alright?" Carlos, the photographer, asks concerned.

"I- that's our baby?" I say louder than I should.

Uncle Douglas, who offered to chaperone this little excursion, laughs. "You're pregnant?" His hands clasp together. "I'm gonna be a Great Uncle!"

I nod, and she touches her belly slightly. "You put that, *here*."

"I-" I stop fishing into my pocket as Carlos starts taking pictures again suddenly. "Since I'm already on my knees." I open the box. "Kaycee Leanne McLane, I've loved you as a friend for fourteen years. Let me call you wife, and I'll love you the rest of my life."

"Oh, my. *Cal...*" She reaches for me. Grabbing my lapels. "Yes! Of course!" She kisses me. The first *real* kiss since before her rape. I stand lifting her up, deepening the kiss a moment.

Not wanting to muss her too much, I put her down and see her makeup isn't even smudged. "They really shellacked it on, huh?" I laugh.

"You're telling me?"

The rest of our prom photos become engagement photos as Carlos starts to focus on the ring.

We arrive at the prom, and it's what you would expect. An overpriced hall with twinkle lights and too many balloons in the school colors. We're handed masks at the door as it's *that* kind of party. Kaycee stands out amongst the crowd in her royal blue gown. So many pink things, whites, and silvers. I was glad she followed her own beat and chose to stand out.

Dinner is a chicken picatta like entrée, with a twice-baked potato and a mixed green salad with honey vinaigrette. Drinks are sparkling ciders, sodas from an old fashioned soda bar plus an assortment of flavored waters and teas.

The theme song is *Love on the Brain*, by Rihanna. It's a little on the nose for me, but they all agreed to it in the Prom committee, so it is what it is.

We dance some, eat more. Then we head out to take the prom backdrop pics. These are sponsored by the photo club. The proceeds this year were going to SARC, to raise awareness, and help with services. It was the school's way to show their support for Kaycee after what happened. The cheerleaders rallied for her, as did the dance team.

Maybe the people here weren't so bad, after all.

Kaycee and I are standing waiting for our

pic when Lenard Criss stops us. "Are you two engaged?" He asks, grabbing Kaycee's hand.

She smirks, unable to play it off. "Yup."

"That's so exciting!" He gets ready to take the picture.

"I'm also having his baby!" She pulls the dress against her, and there it is the thing she's been hiding from everyone, including me. *The Bump.*

Lenard takes the pic and squeals. If we didn't already know, he was gay. "You are my heroes! So brave!" He gushes. "Congrats, guys!"

We walk away, and I am just looking at her.

"What?" She laughs. "I'm past the worry point; this isn't going anywhere. Might as well let everyone in on it."

"You *sure*?"

"Sure as I am that I wanna be your wife for life. Or that I've got a sweet wet spot developing as we speak."

I lick my lips, as the room clamors. The music stops, and the mic gives feedback.

"Good evening, Class of twenty nineteen!" Cira Cummings calls out over the crowd. Hoots and hollers. Someone yells *show me your tits, which* gets a laugh. "No, I'm not doing that! Anyhow, we are all here to have one last hoorah before life happens for *real*. Colleges, jobs, the army for some! We love you, Chuckie Robbins!" She blows a kiss to the senior that started out a slacker, but after basic training became a contender with me academically. "So with that, I have the Prom King and Queen to announce! As you all know, this year's scholarship is one thousand dollars to help with books and supplies for college. How great is that?"

More hoots.

"Alright, so our Queen first, we had an online nomination, and she won by a correspondent landslide. Kaycee McLane! C'mere girlie!"

Kayce looks at me. "Why would I be?"

"Hey, you better go." I smile, kissing her softly.

"What about you?"

"I'll be right here."

"Okay."

"C'mon Kayce! Get your crown and your check!"

I watch as Kaycee goes up on stage. They give her a dozen roses and a cheap plastic crown. Frankly, I liked her tiara better.

She's all smiles and nods while they call out the Prom King.

"Calvin Pennington the Fourth! Come on, Cal, come claim your queen!"

I'm pushed toward the stage. Next thing I know, I'm standing before the whole senior class. Getting a taste of what graduation day is going to be like. They take a few more pics and someone sides, Cira.

"I understand we have reason to celebrate! Not only are these two your king and queen, but they're actually getting hitched, and having a baby!"

We look at each other, in shock. Well, I guess if it was gonna come out, it may as well be all at once.

CHAPTER 28

KAYCEE

Our secret is out. We cut and run after the King and Queen's dance. Heading to this sweet little bed and breakfast, Cal booked for us under Mister and Missus Pennington the fourth. He was so sure I'd say yes. He lifts me at the door, making me laugh outright.

"Easy there, we're not *actually* married."

"I just want to make this night as memorable as I can."

"Cal, ain't' no way I ever forget tonight." I palm his face, as we go inside, I kiss him.

His face is so smooth, and rough at once. The taste of his kiss sends signals to the right parts, and my knees are weak as he puts me down. "Unzip me?"

He grasps the zipper at my side as I unclasp the neck of the gown, it slips down to my middle, revealing the black cropped bustier I got special for tonight.

"Is this the rest of my present?"

"Keep going." I urge him. He pulls the dress down off my filling in hips and is confronted by lacy *crotchless* panties.

He lets out an approving hum, kissing

my panty line. Even though it's starting to be overtaken by this growing belly.

"You popped." He says, his hands caressing me. I tilt my head back; I've missed his more intimate touch.

"Seems that way."

He kisses my navel and gently parts my legs before taking a taste of me. I'm so sensitive I almost come on contact. This is gonna be fun. Getting me to the bed, he sits me down and gets me to open wide so he can indulge himself. I'm sitting up, grasping his head, pulling his blonde locks while he fucks me with his marvelously agile tongue. I come not once but twice in seconds. If this was what they meant by multiple orgasms. YES PLEASE! Laying back, I let him touch me more, use his hands better. He pulls at me, stretches me. Fulfills my aching need to come again.

I'm left covered in sweat and panting as he undresses. Climbing into the bed with me, he gets behind me, opening my legs, so he can come at it from behind. I freeze, a flash of Heath coming into my mind. *Feeling his breath.*

"Hey, I'm here, *you're safe.*" Cal kisses me, and realizing I can't handle that way, he stops. "C'mere." He pulls me onto him, and I help guide him into my center. "Christ, you're so wet."

"Side effect of pregnancy." I moan, holding his hands as I move up and down on him.

"Great side effect." He sits up and starts to suck my tits.

"Easy, they're sore."

"I'm on it." He goes slow and gentle. The motions overthrowing me and making me come again.

Here I am making love to a man who wants me... *Loves me*. Has fought for me and protected me. No wonder I'm a mess, all I've done is made him alienate his family and jeopardize his future with a baby.

"Hey, Kayce, why are you crying?" We stop, and I start to sob.

"It's all too much. You, me. All of this. Who are we kidding? We're gonna fail, and you're gonna resent me forever."

He pulls back, to wrap me into his arms. "Kayce, I love *you*. Not some *idea* of you. I wanted to marry you *before* I found out about the baby. Not *because* of it. You are my lover, my best friend, and partner in crime. Please realize that all I do is *for you*. We have the world on a string and by God! We are gonna tie this bitch up and present our happy life to everyone who's ever knocked it. It's you and me, and baby makes three. From now till the wheels fall off."

"How'd I get so lucky to wind up with a smart guy?"

"Luck nothing; I was smart enough to realize a good thing before I was too late."

"You mean- it?"

"Same difference."

I kiss him softly. "Make love to me?"

"With pleasure."

CHAPTER 29

CALVIN

The night was good. Followed by a pre-dawn session and then breakfast on the balcony. It's finally warmed up, and the rain is holding out until we get home. Or at least that is what the weather person said. But you know how that goes. We're here one more night before going back to reality, and we've decided to explore the local food.

We wind up having a late lunch at a place called *The White Dog Cafe*. It's interesting. I found the place online before we came out. I just knew Kaycee would get a kick out of the place.

"Stetson would hate this." She smiles, sitting across from me. "Everything is puppies."

The upholstery is red velvet, there are kitschy dog statues everywhere you look, and dog head sculptures. Another room has what look like huge empty cans for light fixtures with oversized forks for décor and birdhouses all over.

She gets the Southern Fried Chicken sandwich, and I get the double bacon burger.

It's huge, tender, and worth the doggy bag back to the Inn. We decide that we are gonna take a stroll through the garden. All of the rain through April has everything green with bursts of color. It smells fresh and clean.

"This, it's places like this that I want to take our kid when it's here."

Kaycee holds on to me. "Do you want a boy or a girl?"

"I don't care, so long as it's healthy, has my height and your curls." I give her a gentle squeeze as we find a secluded little bench and sit.

She straddles me with a glimmer of mischief in her eyes.

"Kayce, what are you doing?"

"That spicy pickle made me horny. I need you inside me."

"Can't we- you know, go back to the room first?"

"Too late for that." She hikes up her skirt and unzips my jeans, to start stroking me.

"Ahh, Kayce, this isn't a good-" Fuck it. I grab her ass and let her have her way. She's taking her time and drawing it out to merciless effect when I feel the first raindrop. "It's-"

She silences me with her kiss, as the thunder rumbles and lightning crackles in the distance. The rain starts, and it just encourages her movements. Faster, she moves and does little swivels as she takes me deep.

"Come on." She pants. "Come *with* me," She stares me in the face. Locking on to my eyes, as she starts to come. I see her pupils go wide in her ecstasy. My balls take the kick, and I come. Filling her up. If she weren't pregnant, she certainly would be now.

Finished, for now, we make our way back through the garden, already wet in every conceivable way, running wasn't on the agenda.

***

"I'm hungry!" Kaycee whines as we get off the highway.

"We're almost home, can't it wait?"

She glares at me. "Are you actually saying *no* to me?"

"I uh-*well*... I mean, we literally just ate before leaving PA. How could you possibly be hungry again?"

"Growing another person here." She points to the pooch. "You put it here you, need to keep it fed, or else I get cranky. If I get cranky, you don't get any hanky panky."

"Roger that." I turn off. "Dairy Queen?"

"Mmm. Yes, please."

Not hungry myself, I fall to watching her inhale three chili cheese dogs *and* fries. She's still working on a large strawberry kiwi slush when we pull up to the house. It's quiet, but the van is here, meaning Tracie is home, which is strange because she usually works Sunday afternoons.

Kaycee slurps as I grab our bags and follow her into the house.

"About time, you got back. Don't you ever check messages?" Tracie sounds *very angry*.

"Hi, mom." Kaycee smiles. She's in too

good a mood to be spoiled apparently.

"Don't you, hi, mom me! You announced you're pregnant to the entire Senior Class and a large chunk of my customers!" Oh yeah not angry, livid is more like it.

"You!" She turns on me. "I allow you in my home, take you in. The only thing I truly asked of you to not do. ONLY THING! You go and do!" She starts shaking her head; I look to the living room. Grandpa Compton is sitting in his chair, and he looks at us with such disappointment.

"How-" He stops. "Do you have any idea what it's gonna cost to take care of a baby? You two can't seem to take care of yourselves. How are you gonna keep a kid, safe?"

"I have it all worked out." Kaycee says, still slurping.

I look to her as she takes my hand.

"Do tell Miss-Know-It-All." Tracie quips.

"Well, my store manager already said I could transfer to where ever they have stores. So I'm certainly doing that. I'm getting all my medical right now from Planned Parenthood, and they said I can transfer my info to a Penn facility, so there's that. If you don't wanna carry me on your insurance anymore, which I'd get, I'll apply for state help. There is SNAP and WIC. There's no shame in asking for help. I'll do my online classes first, so I can be home after the baby comes. Maybe I'll look into selling Scentsy or something while I'm doing that. Miss Warner- April has asked me if I want to be a SARA, for the Penn chapter of SARC, and I'm thinking about it. That wouldn't pay very much, but it's got resources and would keep me in my therapy. Cal's gonna be in school and working too so we won't starve. I've even found a few nice houses that are subsidized, right next to the college. We've got appointments to look at those this week. So like I said, I've got it all worked out."

I just let out a little laugh. "So, that's that." I add not sure what else to say.

"It's a better plan than you had at eighteen." Grandpa Compton gruffs. "You- I believe said all you needed was love and dreams."

"Look who's talking, Mister insta love, world traveler." Tracie retorts. "I just- I'm worried."

"Tracie." I go to her. "Look, I'm not your ex. I'm not *Logan*. I didn't know him, but I'd say that we don't have much in common, or you wouldn't have let me be around all these years. Wouldn't have *encouraged* our *friendship*, our *relationship*. I've been here in some capacity for more than a decade. Could you say the same for him?"

Tracie's eyes are welling up.

"I'm a good egg, sure this is sooner than we all would have planned, and we got young and careless, but this is the endgame. Is it not? This is life, what we strive for. A home, family, the person we want to be with for the rest of our lives."

"Mom, it's not gonna be easy, but it doesn't have to be hard either. Not if you guys are involved. Don't shut us out; don't be Pennington's."

I can't help but laugh. "Maybe I should

take your name."

"It's weird, but I'm for it." Kaycee says. "Break the cycle, drop the pompous numbers."

"Maybe." I kiss her softly. "You wanna show off your crown now?"

"Most definitely."

CHAPTER 30

KAYCEE

I'm in Principal Koopersmith's office. Seems my little announcement at Prom was not appreciated.

"Kaycee, you're a looked up to young lady."

"Bullshit, I'm hardly a blip on the radar, but go on if you must."

"That mouth of yours. Can you not control it?'

"Why? You're gonna suspend me, right? Might as well make it worth it."

"We have exams this week; if I were to suspend you, there would be a riot from the parents over the reason. It's just pregnancy is like a sickness, girls *catch* it."

"Uh-huh." I laugh. "Pretty sure that's *not* how it works. There's usually a boy and about thirty seconds of fumbling around if you're lucky. Me? I got *really* lucky."

"Kaycee!"

"What?"

Koopersmith rubs the bridge of his nose in frustration. "Please, can you just not make a spectacle of yourself."

"I can't promise that. I am something of a spectacle in general, you know?"

"Ugh. Just go to class."

"Smartest thing you've said yet." I take my feet off his desk for the fourth time and sling my bag over my shoulder. "Later. Koo-" I stop, feeling a swimming motion in my belly. I grab it. "Oh-wow!"

"Kaycee, are you alright?"

"Yeah, it—just. It moved." I smile. "I—gotta go find Cal."

Heading down the hall and up the stairs to the red wing, I find Cal in Modern Literature. I knock, and Missus Beamer spots me.

"Can we help you?'

"Yeah, can I see Cal Pennington for just a sec?"

"Why? We're in the middle of class, can't it wait?"

I grab my belly. "I don't know."

Cal is up and at the door. "What's wrong?"

I grab his hands and put them on me. "Feel." We wait. "Right there. Feel it?"

He laughs. "Is that?"

"I think so." I smile, as he kisses me I notice a few girls are up and headed for us, as is the teacher. Next thing I know, it's like I'm an amusement park attraction, everyone wants a hand on the belly. I *so*-should be selling tickets.

The next couple of classes go similarly, and the baby doesn't disappoint. Once it started, it was like it wasn't gonna stop. That was until we got in the car and started the ride out to our first apartment appointment. Ten minutes in and poof, no more kicks.

"Guess I know how we'll be putting this little one to bed." I smile.

"Yeah." Cal takes my hand. "We're really doing all this?"

"Yup. You good?"

"I'm great. You?"

"Terrified."

"Oh, thank *God*. I was afraid it was just me." Cal says, relieved.

"We have every reason to be freaked out, but I'd be more freaked out if I wasn't with you." I squeeze his hand.

"Same here. So these houses?"

"Looked pretty good from the pictures? One's fully furnished, I'm on the fence about that, but the other one didn't have much, pic wise. We just gotta go see."

"What's the price range?"

"It doesn't matter. What matters is how much we make. It'll be more at first, but when I go on maternity leave, it'll change. We'll be okay."

"My uncle said he'd help too."

"That will be great. You're gonna go left up here." I point him in the right direction according to the nav system on my phone.

The house is sturdy looking and sorta cream. Six blocks from the college.

Cal leans into me. "It smells like old man." He whispers, then chuckles. "Looks like it too."

The furniture must have been thirty years old, based on patterns. He was right; there was an odor of sorts. The landlady also explained we couldn't have any pets. Well, screw that. I wasn't gonna leave Stetson behind.

"That was horrible." Cal says as we get in the car.

"I know. I'm sorry."

"The other needs to be better."

"I'm praying."

A few blocks away, we park on the street as instructed and walk down a long patch of sidewalk, flanked by all kinds of bushes and trees. Already it's *better*. It's actually private and pretty. There's a two-car garage, but it's got a POD out front, explains the street parking instructions. The place is teal and white plus its two floors. Lots more space.

"What do you think?" I say to Cal.

"Let's get inside before we judge it."

"Right." I'm bouncy. I already want it for the fenced-in yard.

We knock, and a middle-aged woman answers. "Hello? You must be Kaycee and Calvin?"

"Yes." I muscle in past Cal, shaking her hand.

"I'm Gladys, come in. Forgive me; I'm still clearing out. I promise the place will be spotless by the end of the month."

We walk right into the living room, and I'm in love. Hardwood floors and built-in bookshelves. There is a fireplace and an actual dining room next to the kitchen. Not just space to put a table like at home.

"You've got three bedrooms, so I don't know if you all planned on roommates."

"We're bringing one in a few months". I

smile. "Can we paint?" I ask. Holding my belly.

"Oh, my you're having a baby? How exciting? Of course, you can do as you like, within reason. I mean until you've come out of escrow."

Cal looks at me. "Grandpa said he'd call in a favor. Get us a down payment for rent to own. If we liked any."

"Why didn't you tell me?"

"I didn't want to add any pressure, but Cal, I *like* this place."

"So do I."

I smile, "Yeah?"

"It's got potential for us. Room for what we need and for what we may want." We look at Gladys. "Thank you; We'll be in touch with an offer this week."

"Really? That would be wonderful."

CHAPTER 31

CALVIN

Exams, done. House, found. Fiancée, happy. So why am I not sleeping? Oh, that's right, we graduate in twelve hours. In twelve hours! I have to give a speech about life and the future. About accomplishment. About- I have no *fucking* idea. I've been trying to write this thing since I found out I was getting the award. Nothing seems right. My goals are shifting; my dreams are changing. How do I talk about taking off to college and studying when I just want to study my Kaycee's growing belly and not miss a moment of the baby's life? I'm looking forward to being a dad, not an undergrad.

I'm feeling trapped again. Locked into this idea that people have of me, they got over the shock of the mouth. Will they accept me if I tell them that not all futures are laid in stone? Guess I'll find out.

"Hey?" Kaycee drags her leg up against mine and gently scratches my abs. "What are you doing up?"

"I'm not. You are." I smile in the dark.

"I can tell by your breathing. What's

wrong?"

"Just thinking."

"About your speech?"

I squirm as she slips her hand into my shorts. "It's not as good as it could be."

"You just be honest, and it will be great." Her head disappears under the covers, and her belly grazes my thighs as she goes to work on me. My eyes roll back as she sucks and nibbles on me until I'm good and hard, then gets herself onto me.

"Hmm. What if-Ah..." Her wet pussy clenches me, and my brain gets fuzzy. I let the thoughts of the night fade and instead enjoy my woman's body. Her breasts have doubled in size, and their tenderness is easing so I can play with them again. They're heavier now and so much more sensitive. She comes harder, gets wetter more easily. It's like a Slip n' Slide. I love it. Though her voracious need is gonna kill me. We've almost been caught at school. On more than one occasion. She wants to fuck three, four times a day, without fail. Hence these mid-night romps. If I'd been asleep, she'd have woken me for a ride.

Come morning, it will be reverse cowgirl or in the shower, depending on how late we sleep. Sometimes it's both. I'm thinking of getting a mold of my cock made and sending it out to have a dildo or vibrator made for her birthday in September. It may give me a bit of a reprieve.

I come, and she slips off me, gets dressed, and heads for the bathroom. I try and go back to bed, but for all the shit running through my head.

***

Standing in the courtyard at Cradle Bay High, I'm getting ready to go sit on the stage with the rest of the honor roll.

"You look good in that."

I turn hearing my father's voice. "Sir?" I say, surprised. "What are you doing here?"

"I received the invitation from the school."

"I haven't seen you in four months, and you choose *today* to show your face?" My face is bound to be blood red.

"I wanted to see you—it's just your mother."

"Yeah, because she keeps your balls in her purse. I forgot."

"*Son.*"

"Nope. I'm done. *You* don't get to call me that. Letting her do to me what she did. All those *years.*"

"I didn't know what to do."

"Booting her ass would have been a good start." I hear Grandpa Compton before I feel his hand on my shoulder. He's got his prosthetic and though walking with a cane, is at his full five foot ten height.

"You aren't welcome here."

"Back off-old man."

"You really should watch your tongue and respect your elders. We tend to come in packs." Behind him are seven more men, different ages, all looking mean as hell.

My father drops his head. *Bested.*

"Good-bye." I say as Grandpa Compton puts his arm around me.

"See, I told ya we Navy boys, stick together.

I smile. "Thank you."

"Anytime, *son*."

I head up to the stage and sit, looking out over the Senior Class. All one hundred and forty-two of them. Among them, my best friend, my love, *my Kaycee*. She's full-on glowing. With a beaming smile. Our eyes connect. She gives a little finger wave, and I give a short close to the body palm lift as she mouths *I love you*.

I have to sit here as everyone gets their diplomas. I'm going through my speech when they call me. I put it down, get my diploma and back I go. Finally, it's time for my speech. As I go to the podium. "Good afternoon. I—um, I'm Calvin, Cal, as you know." I look over the sea of bored faces. I'm trying to organize my cards when I find a little envelope. I look at Kaycee, and she winks. I covertly open the envelope and am looking at another ultrasound.

"I—uh-excuse me—I just—um." Feedback as I look at the picture. She didn't tell me she had an appointment. Circled on it is a spot, and next to it is one word. *Boy!*

"Boy!" I say louder than I planned, and I get looks. I don't' even care. "We're having a boy."

Kaycee is barely standing when I hop the stage to meet her. Hoots and cheers as she rounds the chairs and is in my arms. I kiss her, then drag her back to the podium.

"Sorry for the interruption, guys. But when you're future calls, you gotta answer." I wrap my arms around Kaycee and our baby we've made. "See, I had this idea in my head about what the future was *supposed* to be. Work hard, make money, be lavish, and well frankly miserable. What's the point of it all if your head is always down and you don't see the world around you? Your life is now. Your future isn't set. It can change in any number of ways at any moment. It's how you adapt to that change that makes or breaks you. We need to stop being so rigid. We need to be more fluid in our lives and more open to the possibilities. Otherwise, we may miss the present while waiting for the future to begin. So my advice to you as you start your next chapter. Stop and actually experience it. Suck the marrow out of it, and enjoy it for tomorrow isn't promised to any of us. But today is guaranteed." I kiss Kaycee again. "Thank you."

They stand. They clap. This includes the adults and the faculty. I was once again the boy they all knew and loved. Accepted, but you know what? I didn't give a damn.

CHAPTER 32

KAYCEE

"Now, you have everything?" Mom questions while I'm getting into the Santa Fe. It's June first and hotter than Jason Moma coming out of the ocean in his birthday suit. I swear the fucking weather is nutso.

"We're good, mom." I kiss her before closing the door to sweet, sweet air conditioning.

The papers for the house were signed right after graduation, and between Grandpa and Cal's Uncle Douglas, it's half paid for already.

Our mortgage, as opposed to rent is just seven hundred a month. With all the water and stuff included. We're in place for help with things like the electric and heat, so we are gonna be good. I'm optimistic. The boy, who of course we're calling Calvin, is growing like a little weed. I've gained a whopping twenty pounds! All in the belly. I swear I look like I'm carrying two babies, not one! Uncle Douglas even gave us gift certificates to JC Penny and Macy's for furniture, so we have a house that feels like a *home*. I got a projector and used it to paint the nursery. We are doing a Calvin and Hobbes theme, because, obviously! The room's going to have tigers all over. Mom made a stuffed one that's safe for him to sleep with right out of the gate as well as receiving blankets. It's all too fucking cute.

I roll down the window. "I'll see you this weekend for lunch, right?"

"Wouldn't miss it." She hugs me again through the window, and Cal gets in.

"You tryin' to freeze me out?" He chuckles, turning down the air.

"Touch that dial, and I'll cut you off!"

"You couldn't if you wanted to." He smirks. "You crave it like you crave chili dogs!"

"Oh! Can we get some on the way?"

Cal laughs. "I suppose. If you're good."

"I'll be a perfect little princess." I answer, reaching over and rubbing his thigh.

"Okay, behave, you two." Mom says, walking away.

"So, the last of the furniture is supposed to meet us at the house?" I ask as we are pulling away.

"Yup. I made the appointment for delivery to match up. We're good."

"I'm excited."

***

"Hey, Kayce?" I'm awoken to Cal's hands on my belly and his gentle kiss on my temple.

I was excited, alright, so excited; I drifted right to sleep!

"Hey, we're home."

Home. It had a whole new meaning. This was ours, no mom or grandpa lying in wait to ambush us. We could forget to do the dishes or have chocolate cake at three in the morning whilst completely naked with no one to see.

As I'm being helped from the truck, I notice movement inside. A curtain swishes.

"What's going on, Cal? Who's here?" I ask.

"Can't get anything by you, can I?" He chuckles. We walk up to the house, and he opens the door. "Welcome to your baby shower."

I instantly tear up seeing all the Calvin and Hobbes decorations. My mom, Grandpa, and Uncle Douglas are in my line of sight first. Then I see Micha and April Warner as well as Wendy and Bonnie from the center. Ciera is here too.

"How'd" I ask whiney and confused.

"We do own a van, and you're soon to be hubby took the long way." Mom smiles, hugging me.

Cupcakes, and cookies it's all themed. Balloons, diaper cakes. More stuff for the nursery.

"April, I can't believe you guys came." I hug her.

"We took a donation around the center. Here's a two thousand dollar gift certificate to Target, for the baby and you. I hope it helps."

"I-thank you so much!" I'm a blubbering mess. I see that Uncle Douglas and my mom are getting familiar. That will be sorta weird if it goes anywhere, but whatever makes mom happy. Noise machines, bouncers, playpens. It's all here. As is a chili cheese dog spread fit for a Queen, like me. These people know me too well.

It's well after nine when they all finally go. Mom insisted on staying until every dish was cleaned and every bag of trash on the road.

"I just want to sleep. I think I had one too many chili dogs. I'm sorta gassy." I burp, loudly as I come into our living room. I love that idea. *Ours*. Cal is half asleep on the couch. *Our couch*. He laughs quietly as I plop next to him. "Wanna have sex?" I say half enthused.

"Do we have to?" He whines.

"No."

"Good, cause I was afraid you might blow me away with another chili burp."

"Jerk-face." I punch his arm as he wraps it around me.

"C'mere. Just don't breathe on me." I, of course, retaliate by breathing hard and heavy in his face. He tries to avoid it. "Oh-no-that's-horrible!" He laughs as I climb on him, pinning him down for a good bit of kissing.

We find our second wind and manage to shrug out of our clothes. I'm now riding him on the couch like the rodeo champ that I am. He's got to come at me from the back now because the belly is getting in the way of my clitoral stimulation otherwise. I miss the eye contact, but he makes up for it with lots of kisses in between. We don't last long, but we also don't have to worry about going anywhere and just settle where we are. Happy and content.

"One room down." I whisper as he starts to snore.

"Six to go." He mumbles back, kissing the top of my head

CHAPTER 33

CALVIN

"Cal? Look at her! We have to go get her!"

We've hit month seven, and the so-called nesting has started. When she's not at work, where they are keeping her well-stocked in plain crullers and me in turkey sausage and coffee, she's had me rearranging the house, and now she's convinced we need a *dog*. As if Stetson wasn't animal enough.

I've never been keen on dogs. Probably because I've been chased by my fair share being a bike rider. Yes, I'm still using my bike. It leaves the Santa Fe available to Kayce for whatever she needs. Today it appears she needs an eight-month-old American Staffordshire, pitbull mix named Abby.

"She's only one ten to adopt. She's altered and microchipped already. *Please?*"

"Where is she?"

Kayce hops up, holding her belly, excitedly. "Over at PAWS on Grays Ferry Ave. Literally like ten minutes up the road."

"We'll go *look*."

"Thank you!" She kisses me, and little Calvin gives a hard kick. He's taking up a lot of space now. She waddles off to go get dressed. I look at Stetson. "Guess you're getting a sister."

He yowls in protest at me.

"Yup, I agree."

We get to the PAWS facility, and sure enough, this puppy is fucking *adorable*. Big yellow eyes, floppy ears, lanky as all hell as she's practically tripping over herself to get to us. Kayce bends down to meet her and winds up on the floor.

"You okay?"

"I'm fine." She assures me, getting puppy kisses. "Yup, look at her, she's perfect. Why someone would give her up."

"They were afraid she would get too big." The volunteer offers.

"Nonsense, we got a big yard, we can handle her."

"She's good with cats, other dogs, children." The volunteer smiles.

"Good, we'll be having all that."

"Will we?" I ask, unsure.

"Oh, yes. I want at least four dogs. Four is good, so someone can always have a playmate."

"You know Abby has begun to bond with an older male here. Titan, he's a Sheppard retriever mix. About three years old, but very sweet. If you take them both, we could work something out, I'm sure." The volunteer is now grinning.

Kaycee looks up at me and nods yes with her huge grin.

"It's a lot. Two dogs, the cat, *and* the baby?"

"We can handle it. Besides, it'll keep me busy. You get to go to work; you start school in just about a month. I'd rather get them now and have them used to the house before mom, and the fam comes back for the fourth."

"Are we actually doing that? I thought it was just talk." I remember it being mentioned at the baby shower, but now that the holiday was about a week away, I had no idea.

"Why else do you think I bought all that meat?"

"Sale?"

"Silly rabbit." She baby talks looking at Abby as the attendant comes back with a huge yellow dog. "This must be Titan." Abby jump kicks to her friend, and Kaycee holds her belly.

"Hey. You okay?" I ask as she grabs on to me and stands.

"Yeah, just a little harder hit than I'm used to."

"You sure?"

"Yeah. We're good." She assures me. Kissing my cheek. "Let's get the paperwork done and get these two home."

Stetson is not a happy cabbage. He took off upstairs as soon as Abby and Titan came in. They are sniffing around while Kaycee and I make dinner. It's too hot to cook indoors, so I'm using the new grill Uncle Douglas shipped us. I had to put it together, but it has been worth it. Cast iron grill plates, a smoker, and a propane burner. I'm making chicken and beef kebabs with peppers, zucchini, and eggplant. It sounds weird, but it's how she likes it right now.

"Oh, you know what? I think I want chocolate mint and banana ice cream."

"You and your weird combos."

Grandpa Compton got us an ice cream maker, and she has gone to town with the cravings.

"Hey, you liked the Peanut butter caramel, marshmallow, apple craze."

"That was *almost* normal." I chuckle, turning the kebabs. Titan and Abby push by Kaycee and take off into the yard. "They seem happy."

Kaycee's hands wrap around me. "Thank you. For them." She hugs me as tightly as the belly now allows. I feel kicking.

"Has he been active like that all day?"

"Yeah, on and off. It's my new normal. Don't look at me like that. I'm fine. I'll worry if he *stops* moving."

"I just-I don't know how this works, and you have most of your appointments without me."

"You work. Look, I have another ultrasound tomorrow. You wanna come? I know you were gonna go register for classes, but maybe you can do *both*?"

"I can register next week. What time?"

"Eleven thirty. I was gonna meet mom for lunch at one. Wanna come to that too?"

"No, you two have some time together. But I'll pay for lunch and even send you off for a mani-pedi."

"You are such a wonderful man." She kisses me. "I love you. Have I told you that?"

"Not today."

"Well, I've said it now."

***

"So everything is looking fine. Your blood pressure is a little high. Have you been indulging in fatty foods? High salts that sort of thing?"

The doctor asks Kaycee as we are sitting in her office. Seeing little Calvin was amazing. He looks like we could hold him now. Though he's still got growing to do, the doctor estimates he's gonna be about twenty-two inches and eight to nine pounds!

"I'm a hotdog addict, doc." Kaycee answers plainly.

"Well, you need to slow down. Kaycee, I see you have already signed all the papers to allow drugs and a C-section if need be. This way, there's no need to have the discussion during delivery. If something goes sideways, it's taken care of."

"What could go sideways? No one tells me anything." I ask, concerned.

"Any number of things. But we don't worry about that. Delivery is a safe thing; women have been having babies since the beginning of time. This has been an easy pregnancy I don't foresee an issue so long as we get that blood pressure down."

"If we don't?"

"We'll cross that bridge when we get to it."

"I'll cut out the fried foods, and the hotdogs. Anything else I need to do?"

"I would suggest you stop working, you

mentioned a bit of spotting, at your last appointment. Let's try to keep Calvin in place as long as possible. So while you don't have to *actually* be in bed, I don't want you on your feet ten hours a day either. You get me?"

"Yes, doc."

"Spotting? Should I be concerned?"

"No, Cal. It's normal as she approaches the end of her term to see a bit of blood and mucus. Though I will advise if you're still having sex that you keep that simple too, no more of you on top, no matter how much you may prefer it. I have a booklet on safer positions for pregnant sex. It may help." The doc hands us a little manual.

I take it. "Hey, whatever works, right?"

Kaycee turns red. "Thank you."

"I'll see you after the holiday. We'll have the genetic tests back by then."

"Sounds good."

We walk out, and I'm looking at the pamphlet. "We can *so*-do all of these, in the Santa Fe, like right now. No problem."

"You are such a perv."

"And you know you love it."

"I knew I didn't put my panties back on for a reason."

CHAPTER 34

KAYCEE

July fourth. The house is decorated, and the people we love are here. I spent the last week with Hareem, the baker from my Dunkin'. He's been teaching me what he knows about baking. I mean, I knew how to make the doughnuts, and all that at Dunkin' but like pastries and cookies? *Not* my thing.

I've got cupcakes filled with red, white, and blue sprinkles, a cake, and all manner of fruit and veggie plates that resemble flags as well as Jello and dips. There are ribs on the grill, burgers, and I made these turkey corn dogs that are *so-* good. I'm lying in the yard in my new swing watching as Micha, Cal, and Uncle Douglas argue about the amount of shock to put in the new pool. I ordered it last week from home depot and paid to have it put together and filled. I was sick of being hot and feeling like a beached whale. They say the water will be good for me. If they ever figure it out, that is.

"We got it!" Uncle Douglas hollers.

"That's good, baby!" Mom yells, and the cat is out of the bag. My mom is doing my soon to be Uncle-in-law.

"Really, mom?"

She shrugs. "Guess the apple rolled toward the tree?" She laughs, taking a sip of her mocktail. "So, dogs?"

"I wanted something that made me feel safer, for when Cal's not around."

"I get it. That's a big boy there."

"Yup."

"They listen?"

"To us, both, which is good. Me a bit more, but I'm here more."

"He's working a lot?"

"Right now. Trying to put in as much as he can so he can stay with us a bit after Calvin comes. I think he's worried about post-partum. You know, since I have issues since the rape."

"Are you still going to the meetings?"

I nod. "When I can. It's getting harder."

"Yeah, I can see that. He's taking you over, isn't he?"

"It's okay, though. We're healthy. I'm a bit tired, but good, otherwise."

"Bless you. I had such a hard time with you. Morning sickness half the time. Most horrific food aversions, couldn't stomach your dad's cologne. Forget Grandpa's Old Spice! I was just miserable the whole time. But when they put you in my arms, it was all worth it." Mom sniffs, her hand to her stomach. "I need to tell you something."

"What's up?" She sounded serious suddenly.

"Well..."

***

"Are you *sure*?" Calvin asks me. I have just pulled him onto the house to tell him the insane thing my mom told me.

"She is. She's seen her doc. Six weeks along, and she's keeping it."

"Does Uncle Douglas know yet?"

I shake my head. "She's afraid to tell him. Afraid he'll be scared off."

"I mean having a baby? At her age?"

"She's only thirty-six."

"Whose having a baby?" Uncle Douglas comes in, for what looks like a refresher on his drink.

We look at him then each other. "I um..." I can't think fast enough, and Cal just looks outside at my mom. I smack him.

"What? I'm not gonna lie?"

I see Uncle Douglas twitch. He puts down his drink and heads outside. We watch, unable to look away as he goes straight for my mom. They exchange a few words, and my mom holds her stomach. Then he touches her too. A wide smile on his face, as he lifts her. Kissing her. My Grandpa smiles, watching with a short little nod.

"He's always wanted a family," Cal says to me. "Just never met a woman he wanted to have one *with*."

"How will that work? Are these kids cousins or what?"

"Calvin will be cousin *and* nephew. We have officially gone into the *weird*." Cal wraps his arms around me. "So be it, Sister Wife."

"Oh, *GOD*!" I cover my face.

"Save that for later. I wanna break in the pool tonight."

"Why Mister Pennington," I say as he grabs my ass and kisses me. "You *are* getting awful fresh."

***

Call me Kevin McAlister for how often I find myself home alone. Sick of just watching the doggies run rampant, I decide I want a snack. Looking through the fridge, I find nothing that I want. I want a box of munchkins damnit. I put on my flip flops and am about to grab the car keys when the doorbell rings. *Who the fuck?* Titan and Abby are barking their heads off as I go to the door. Looking through the curtain first, I see an unexpected face.

"Mister Pennington?" I open the main door, but not the screen one which I keep locked.

"Kaycee." He looks at me, with a half-smile. "Can we talk?" He holds up a box of munchkins and what looks like iced teas. *Bribes.* Damn him for having what I crave.

I hesitate, but know if I need it, Titan will eat his ass. I tell the pups to stand down, and they get quiet.

"Come in." I open the door, praying he can behave.

"You look good. Are you getting enough to eat? Seeing a good doctor?"

"I'm fine. What do you want?"

"A relationship with my son, but I'll settle for one with my grandchild."

"I can't just give you that."

"I've filed for divorce. She's gonna get half, plus, but it's worth it if it will mend this broken relationship. I never should have kept quiet for so long. Never should have allowed her to manipulate me as she has."

"That's on you, Sir. It has nothing to do with me."

"It does, though. I owe you a great apology. You were often done a great injustice in my presence, often by my own actions. See I thought-"

"Oh, I know what you thought. You made that all real clear. Let me make something *real clear* now. I love your *son.* You? I don't give a *flying fuck* about. If you drop dead tomorrow, I will only mourn that it wasn't sooner. I will stand by Cal when you go but will take pleasure in knowing that the world is less one. Less one bigoted megalomaniac, who never realized just how much his children should have mattered. That the legacy he was so worried about was right in front of him. I love Cal, but I hate that I have to take your name." I stand. "Now, kindly leave. Or I shall have to have the dogs remove you. A piece at a time."

"I never."

"You just have."

"Fine, good luck raising that little bastard. Seeing as my son still hasn't married you... Ever wonder why? I taught him it's easier to get rid of girlfriends than wives."

CHAPTER 35

CALVIN

"Cal! Wake up!" Kaycee shoves me out of a perfectly dead sleep.

"Kayce what's wrong, is it the baby?" I sit up.

"No, he's fine. It's just. 'Bout your dad. I can't stop thinking about him being here. I'm afraid he might do something horrible like call child services when Calvin is born or something."

"I don't think he'd go that far." I rub her arms; she's actually trembling. "Kayce, calm down, we're safe. We're gonna be just fine."

"I think we need to get married. Sooner than we talked about."

"Wait- I thought we were gonna wait till after Calvin came?"

"I don't want him born a bastard."

"A bast- Where *is* this coming from?" I ask so confusedly.

"Why are we even waiting? Do you not really want to? Is your father, right? Are you stalling?"

"Listen to yourself? My *Father*? You are taking anything he said at face value? You told him to go, and fucking slink off to die of course he had to come back with something evil to say. I *love* you."

"Then marry me!" She sobs. "But don't make me take your name!"

"So you want to get married, and you want me to give up my legacy? My name and take yours?"

She sniffs. "Y-Yes."

I give her a half roll of my eyes. "I can do that."

She throws herself at me. Kissing me. "I love you! I love you so fucking much!"

"Enough to let me go back to sleep?" I ask through kisses.

"Okay, but we're getting married before you start school."

"That's like two and a half weeks!"

"Three."

"Let's wait for a little, just until September. It'll be a little cooler. You'll be more comfortable."

"I'll be ready to pop!"

"Not quite, besides, it gives us time to actually plan something. Do you just want to go to the courthouse, or would you like to actually have a wedding?"

"Wedding." She pouts.

"I thought so. Tomorrow I'll call Uncle Douglas and your mom. I'm sure they will be able to help, seeing as they're planning a Christmas wedding."

"Okay." She trails her fingers up my thigh. "I wanna play."

"You're gonna be the death of me." I say as she yanks my shorts off me.

****

Morning comes, and Kaycee has my phone going before I even have my coffee beans ground. She's got a video conference working between Tracie and Uncle Douglas.

"Mom, I'm gonna need all kinds of help. I'm thinking it's early autumn, so apples! I want an apple cake and candy apples and a pretty fall tablescape but not that rustic cray, cray. Something elegant. *Pretty*."

"Slow down, little girl. It's too early." Tracie whines.

"I'll send out a planner. Faye can be there by this afternoon if that works for you." I hear Uncle Douglas, chuckle.

"Oh my God, really? That fast?" Kaycee sounds jubilant. "Thank you!"

"Least I can do for my soon to be Stepdaughter. Now go-*relax*. Take a shower and get dressed for the day."

"Thank you. Bye, guys!" She hangs up and is grinning like nothing I've ever seen.

"You look mightily pleased with yourself." I say, savoring the smell of my coffee brewing.

"I'm quite pleased, and you know what that means?"

"I can sleep normal hours tonight?"

She smirks, walking over to me. Pulling her nightgown off. "It means *you* get *pleased*." Pulling up the kitchen stool, she sits down and pulls me to her.

"What is in your pretty little head?"

I was thinking of trying something out."

I raise a brow. Watching as she strokes me and licks me. I'm hard quickly, and then she takes the honey on the counter and drizzles it on my cock, before licking and sucking again. Next thing I know, she's got my cock between her tits and is sucking the tip at the same time.

"Fuck me, that-" I grab her by the head and titty fuck her as she opens her mouth, sucking me.

She backs off. "God, I'm so wet." She brings up her fingers, and they're sticky with her cum. I stop with her tits and dive straight for her pussy. Lifting her off the stool. I get her on the counter, drizzle the honey on her and suck it off her tits. The sweetness is mixed with something salty. I pull my head back and squeeze, realizing she's begun to leak.

"Hey, don't stop, that felt incredible." She moans.

"Your *leaking*."

"I know, it started yesterday. Just go for it. *Please*, they're so tight now."

I lick, and it's a little strange but *not*. I squeeze, and more comes out, trickling down her ripened breast. I guess it's only fair. She's swallowed enough of my cumshots. I go back to sucking and fucking. Breast milk and pussy. The breakfast of champions.

CHAPTER 36

KAYCEE

"You said apples?" Faye the New York-born wedding planner asks, clicking her stylus pen against her tablet. She's in a black pencil skirt slit up to her neck and a flowy purple blouse with what has got to be fake tits on full display. Her hair is fire engine red with lips to match.

"It's what's in my head. Why is it bad?"

"No, I mean, are we talking Snow White princess or something more-situationally appropriate?"

"Such as?" I watch her as she swipes her screen.

"Well, I know you said nothing too rustic, but why not a local orchard? We nix the burlap, bring in formal linens, and arrange beautiful florals using the locals to keep prices down." She swipes some more. "Ah, there's a gorgeous one right here in your county *and*-they do weddings. They have an opening on September fifteenth. But we have to take it now if you want it."

"My birthday is the fourteenth," I confess.

"All the better. Let you get pampered, you and baby. What do you say?"

"We can keep it in the budgets?"

"Douglas has been quite generous." She smiles. "I'll call them now. Here look around. See what you like."

I'm left with a tablet and a head full of ideas. She started a Pinterest board. She's got sections for dresses and shoes, makeup. Groomsman stuff. Flowers, table settings.

"I'm supposed to fill these?" I squeak.

Faye nods. "Oh, honey, have fun with it! Go wild!"

"Go wild?" I whisper. I just wanted a simple, pretty day.

***

"The woman is crazy!" I whine to Cal, laying my head in his lap, flopping on the couch next to him.

"She's going by what you asked for. How is that crazy?" He strokes my hair, pulling it gently across his thighs. "You need a trim."

"Shush you, I like it getting long, straightens it out."

"My point exactly." He bends down, kissing my forehead. "So, we are booked for the weekend of your birthday then?"

"Mmhm." I close my eyes. What he's doing is super relaxing. "That feels good."

"Does it?" I feel his other hand as it starts to unbutton my top.

"What are you up to?" I smile.

"Shenanigans." He passes the pad of his thumb across my nipple. Sending a rush right to my girly bits.

"*Cal...* I'm tired. Bloated, and my feet are the size of tractor tires."

"I got this." He puts the big pillow under me as he kneels on the floor. Crawling down the length of the couch, he grabs my foot and pulls off my ever-tightening socks.

"Hey, what are you-" My eyes roll into the top of my head as he thumbs my instep. "Oh, *God*!" My toes curl, and my back arches to his touch.

"I *said...* I got it."

"*Yes...* You do." I smile as he rubs the foot and calf up to the knee. First, the left then the right. Still, on the floor, he kisses up my legs. Turning me, so my ass is half off the couch, he gets my knees on his shoulders and pulling down my panties, opens me up.

I let out a ravenous moan as he starts in on my dripping pussy.

"Oh, I love this effect of you pregnant." He pants from between my thighs. "It's like a ripened peach. You taste so fucking good."

I pull up my skirt; my belly keeps me from being able to watch him. But I can feel his fingers as they fuck me slow and deep, his tongue focused solely on my swollen clit.

I come in unending waves. He stops only long enough to pull me to the floor so he can take me. With the pillow under the belly, he's got the perfect angle to thrust and really hits the mark.

Just as I come again, I hear the front door pop open, and the dogs go nuts from the yard.

"Baby? It's mom? Are you-Oh My!"

I'm trying to straighten myself while Cal pulls up his pants, but it's too late. Thanks to our big picture mirror, Mom has *seen* the goods.

"You didn't lock the door?" I whimper, redder than an apple at Cal and my mom.

"I'm sorry, baby, I used the hide-a-key, I called, but you didn't answer. I thought you were having a nap." Her face is redder than mine.

"Um, no!"

"Well, I can see that! Can't you-I don't know-use a bed like normal, respectable people!"

"Too much bounce on the belly." Cal answers.

My head swivels toward him faster than Linda Blair in the *Exorcist*. "You didn't just tell my mother that." I deadpan.

"What? She asked a question." He snickers.

"Is this going to be what dinner is going to be like?"

"Oh, mom, I forgot."

"A forty-minute drive, reservations, and I'm gussied up; you had better go get yourself cleaned up before Douglas gets here. You have an hour. It should be plenty of time." Mom insists.

"Where are we going?"

"To Delphine's a little French place that Douglas wants me to try for the wedding. You promised to be taste testers."

I look at Cal, who shrugs. "Free dinner and dessert."

"You've had enough dessert, young

man."

"Yeah? Well, he's about to get a bit more, who do you think washes my hair nowadays?" I stick out my tongue as I take his hand, and we head for the shower.

CHAPTER 37

CALVIN

French food. I've come to the conclusion that I only like three kinds of *French food*. *French Onion Soup, French Dip sandwiches,* and *French Fries.* Kaycee was disappointed that she couldn't touch the cheese platter, but by the time Tracie and Uncle Douglas get married, she can have all the Brie and Neufchâtel she wants.

Tracie seemed to like the rustic feel and little samples on tiny pieces of toasted baguette. I was over it the moment we walked in. I always hated coming to these frou-frou places with my parents.

"Cal?" Kaycee whispers to me in the backseat of the car that took us all.

I take her hand, giving it a squeeze. "Yeah?"

"I don't want that kind of cray-cray for the wedding. Can we do it more simple, but stay pretty?"

"I hope so." I bring her hand up to kiss, and she smiles, putting her head on my shoulder to nap for the ride home.

***

I don't know how others do it. Balance work, school, *and* home life without exploding. I've been going to classes all week while working at night. It's hard to keep my face from falling into the plate for the hour I'm home in-between. Kaycee is left asking me about the wedding, and I find I have no recollection of the conversation minutes after it occurs. I know she's frustrated, in more ways than one. She tried to initiate sex this morning, and I was just so tired. I mean she got me going, that wasn't the problem. I just kept nodding off. You can guess how that went over.

The idea of getting her that mold of my cock keeps looking like a better and better idea. It's nine-thirty, and I'm leaning against the counter at my Verizon Store. It's about all that's holding me up at the moment.

"Dude, you like need a bump or something?"

I look at Brynn, my manager. "Huh?"

"A bump, ya know a toot, a *line*." She makes a snorting sound.

"Um, no, Ma'am, I don't *do* drugs." I laugh, awkwardly.

"You're an eighteen-year-old guy with a full-time job, school, and a kid on the way. How the fuck do you keep up?"

My eyes drop. "I- I'm-not."

Brynn reaches into her bra, coming over to me. "Look, we got more than two hours left. It's dead in here, let's go, do a bump, and then we can play with the phones." She smirks.

"I- well-"

"It's no big deal, like downing a pot of coffee *without* all the sugar. And it won't stain those pearly white teeth of yours."

The rest of the night is a blur. I come to it with Kaycee wrapped round me. *What the hell happened?* I remember feeling like I could take on the world. It was like the night we... When I-my cock is hard as a rock, and she's taking every merciless inch, I have to give.

"Oh, *Cal*." She mewls like a bitch in heat as I plow her from the back. I don't know how long we've been at it, but I spy the clock, and it's after three. Christ, have I come at *all*?

She's dripping so much sweat and cum down her thighs that I'm sticky with it, as I've got a handful of her curls wrapped in my hand. What the fuck am I doing? We don't do this. Not *like* this. I pull out, and she collapses.

"God, Cal... That was..." Her eyes flutter as her legs tremble. She's still touching herself as I head for the bathroom to get her a towel. Checking myself in the mirror, I see my iris' are black. I look like a fucking demon.

Well, I certainly can't do *that* again.

***

Coke is a versatile drug. Did you know you can liquefy it and make candy out of it? Neither did I until Brynn gave me a pack of lozenges. Just one of these little jollies, and

I'm hyper-focused, alert, and able to get whatever I need done. I'm acing classes, selling hard at work, and fucking my girl like a pornstar. Hashtag *winning*. Why then do I feel like a cheat? When I come down, I feel like the lowest of pigs. Some of the things I've done to Kaycee recently...

"She loves me, that's for sure." I say to Brynn, as we're stocking the back room.

"There's nothing wrong with taking a money shot for a guy. It's actually really good for the skin." She says with a smirk." I love a cumshot, especially if I've brought it on with my tongue."

"Oh, Kaycee's gotten a bit too big to be doing *that* anymore."

"Oh, honey." I feel a hand cup my balls. "You must be feeling *very* neglected."

I freeze up, swallowing. "Brynn, what are you doing?"

I feel her hot breath on my neck. "You owe me for the coke." She squeezes me, getting my attention.

"I-you know I've got a fiancée."

"She doesn't need to know how you pay for your habits."

I shrug her off. "It's not a *habit*."

"Tell yourself that. I'll be right here when you run out."

CHAPTER 38

KAYCEE

I'm dying. This has got to be the hottest August in my life. I'm lying in front of the air with ice packs totally naked, and I'm still sweating like a suckling pig on the spit. Mmm, that sounds *really* good, except it's too fucking hot to cook anything. I'm practically living on protein shakes and frozen smoothies right now as I'm too big to drive safely, and I'm too lazy to cook. The heat index is too high to even use my new pool! I'm so disappointed. The dogs are miserable; poor Stetson is hiding under the bed.

The doorbell rings. Ahh, food. Cal is home for a change. He called off from his morning shift, wasn't feeling too good. He does look a little worn for the wear. I mean he's running like the terminator. School, work, taking care of me in *every* way. He's been a little rough, but my GOD was it worth it. I've never come like that before. It's like he's possessed or something. My body aches in places I didn't know it could. Today though, he's snappy. I'm chalking it up to being overworked because if it continues, I'm gonna have to smack him silly. A woman can only take so much, and I'm a *pregnant woman*, so I'm not going to take it nearly as long. I swear if he tries cumming on my face one more time... I'm gonna bite him.

"Kaycee, you're wings are here, so is the cookie dough." Cal comes into the bedroom, and I'm so thankful they've made safe to consume cookie dough. It's all I've wanted for days.

"Thank you. Are you hungry?"

"Nah. I'm gonna go for a shower. See if I can cool down. Then I'm gonna study for a bit downstairs."

"Okay." I say through a mouthful of chocolaty goodness.

I'm lying here with a full belly and a sugar high when I hear the front door pop. Getting up, I see Cal get in the Santa Fe.

Hmm, wonder where he's off to?

CHAPTER 39

CALVIN

Three days. Three days without a lozenge, or a hit of any kind. I'm shaky and short-tempered. Brynn has been watching me withdraw in a gleeful temper. *I hate her.* I hate myself. I need to level off. Just a little taste. A few grams to take the edge off. Cold turkey never did anyone, any good.

I drive out to the address she gave me. It's just past West Philly High School. A whopping ten minutes up the road. I'm hoping that this goes over smoothly. I've got the money she asked for so it should be fine.

Right?

I knock on the door to the *normal-looking* house, and she answers. *Jean cutoffs and a tank.* Thank God. I was afraid I was walking into her in a teddy or some other crazy *sex* stuff.

"There you are. Was thinking you were gonna welch on me."

"Do you have it?"

She opens the door. "Inside, sugar."

I look in; it seems safe enough. Going in, she locks the door, and I'm led to the living room. It's super cool inside. She's got central air. It's nice.

There it was. My snow-white friend. Only it wasn't in a baggie; it was cut and lined up on the table just waiting to be devoured.

"I don't like to snort. You know that."

"This is what I got right now. My guy comes in thirty. Can you wait?" She shrugs, going to the floor and taking a little straw, she starts a line. Tossing her head back, she laughs, with a little snort. "Oh, it's good."

I drop my bag and kneel beside her as she offers the straw. Fuck it; I need the fix.

Up it goes, burning the shit out of my nose and throat. "Ahh, fuck." I complain, then it hits me. The buzzing, it starts in my ears and works its way out. I swallow and adjust my eyes as she leans me down for another one. It goes easier.

"There, baby, isn't that *nice*?" She coos, stroking my thigh. I look down, and she's unbuttoning my pants. I go to stop her, but my hands are heavy. "Just relax. Let me take care of you."

I fall back as she takes off that tank to reveal no bra covering her tits. I chuckle as she wraps her full lips around my cock.

"Oh-that's-*nice*." I say as my eyes flutter into the back of my swimming head.

When next I regain my senses, my cock is slathered in lube, and I'm balls deep in Brynn's ample ass. It's tighter than anything I've ever had and fuck if it doesn't feel great.

"Yeah, baby!" She hollers, backing up against me, slamming hard, her ass cheeks slapping against my thighs. I'm not alone with her. Under her is a *guy*. We're all covered in sweat. I feel the guy's cock in her, rubbing me, and getting my load ready to blow. "Cum in me! Cum in my ass, cum in my pussy! Make a fucking mess of me!" She groans, and the filthy way she demands it makes me do it. I pull out to finish it on her back, and she squeals in delight.

My cock doesn't want to go down, though. "Fuck, why won't this shit go away?"

"That's the coke, baby, now let's clean it up so you can pound my pussy again."

"N-No! I can't- I shouldn't have done this."

"Yeah, well, the last hour says differently."

"Yeah buddy, you came in her ass and her mouth already, what's one more hole?"

"Are you crazy? Or trying to get knocked up?" I shake my head.

"Baby, I ain't got those parts no more. So I'm just a vessel to be filled. Now, if you want your fix, you're gonna *earn* it." Brynn snaps. Using baby wipes to clean herself up.

"I'm not. In fact, I'm gone."

"See you soon." She wiggles her fingers at me as I slam the door.

I get to the car, and I'm freaking out. What have I done? Fucked a tramp. A skeezy one at that, and my boss. How am I supposed to work and shit now? Speaking of work, I have to be there in an hour. I need to get home and clean this ass of mine and not alert Kaycee.

I need all the luck I can get.

***

I try and promise myself that I can resist the powder, that I can resist that slutty boss of mine. I am a liar and a cheater. I deserve to be punished. So I let Brynn punish me.

I'm in the back room while she digs her heels into my back, her wet snatch a perfect place to bury my hard cock. She sprinkles a bit of coke on me and then has me fuck her. Holy shit, not only is my cock numb, but it's harder than it's ever been. It's great because it gives me the added oomph to meet Kaycee's demands when I get home. I wash up, of course. I'm not a *monster*.

"We're getting married this weekend. You know this has to stop, right?" I say to Brynn as I'm fixing my pants.

"Yeah, you keep saying that. Yet here we are again."

"No, I mean it. I need to pay another way or get help. Something *else*."

She kisses my cheek. "Sure, baby. Whatever you say."

CHAPTER 40

KAYCEE

"I'm gonna be sick." I run for the bathroom of the bridal suite at the Orchard. It's not long before I'm to walk down the aisle, and I can't stop my stomach from rolling.

I hardly slept. They took me away from Cal at lunch yesterday, and I haven't seen him since. I know he's here *somewhere*, but no one will let us talk. I've had my phone taken away too, so no phone communication either.

"It's okay to be nervous." Mom assures me as Faye comes over and gives me a ginger mint.

"It'll kill nausea and your breath. Just suck on it after you swish and spit."

I nod. "How does everything look?"

"Just beautiful. Your guests are all eager to see you." Faye smiles, as she and mom help me to stand.

"You ready to put on the dress?" Mom asks me, and I swallow, with a short nod.

"Do you think he's gonna like it?"

"Based on what you got on under here? I think he's gonna love it." Mom blushes. "I have a few things for you." She holds out a pale blue pearl necklace. "It was grandma's; it's been passed down. For each wedding. So it's got you covered for something old, borrowed and blue, as for something new, I hoped you'd accept these." She opens a box with a pair of diamond and sapphire hoops. "From Douglas and I."

"Oh, Mom." I gasp, overwhelmed.

They pull me together, and I slip on my dress. An empire waist, with silver embellishments at the underbust and a sweetheart neckline. Putting my new boobs totally on display. My hair is in a half pony with my curls full and trailing down my back. In it is baby's breath and blue roses, courtesy of the Cradle Bay Science club, who, as I understand, is in attendance as is the cheerleading squad, the dance team, and half the faculty of our former school. Leave it to my mom. I invited some of the group, and since I am marrying my best friend, I asked April to be my maid of honor. She's been helping to keep me from running away from all this and eloping.

"You look perfect." April smiles. "I'll tell them five minutes, okay?"

I swallow, trembling. "Okay."

I walk out to the hall and am met by my grandpa. He's gotten good enough with the prosthetic that he's gonna walk me down the aisle *without* the cane.

"You ready, Seabee?" He says softly, taking my arm and handing me my apple and cranberry bouquet.

"As I'll ever be." Wagner's March starts,

and so do we.

The chairs are set up in a horseshoe to see us better under the apple trees. There is a long red carpet for us to follow, and to either side are red, orange, and white mums in beautiful stone planters. Uncle Douglas stands as Best Man and April as Maid of honor. Ciera, along with Bonnie and Wendy, are bridesmaids all in lovely chocolate and candy apple red chiffon dresses. Micha, Joey, and Walter, guys from Verizon that work with Cal are in Chocolate suits with candy apple red ties and boutonnieres. It's bigger than I thought or planned, but it's perfect. Cal stands at the end of the carpet, on a small landing under a bough of apples. His beige suit standing out against all the greenery. His tie is chocolate. He looks wonderful with his hair pulled back, and his glasses- His glasses are gone. I bite my ruby lip, hesitating.

"It's okay." Grandpa gives me a nudge as I make eye contact with Cal.

I take a deep breath, and I'm handed off to the man that would be my husband.

CHAPTER 41

CALVIN

It's perfect. Her hand in mine. Our hands joined. Our worlds connected. The only problem is I'm a dirty, lying, cheating snake and coward who is too afraid to tell her the truth. I'm addicted to coke and *fucking* my supplier. I don't know anyone else to get it from. It's not like I can just be like *hi, I'm looking for some coke*. That's how you get mugged or shanked. I'd prefer neither of those things. Walter is a possible source. I invited him to the wedding, hoping he and I could come to an agreement that didn't involve a cock getting sucked.

We've said our vows and signed the papers. I'm officially changing my name to Calvin Archer McLane, and little Calvin, when he's born, will be the beginning of a new legacy. *Mine*. He will be Calvin Archer McLane Jr. Kaycee did an awesome job with Faye for the set up of the place. It's beautiful. All hardwood, roaring fires, inside and out, full soda bars since most of the guests are underage and the food? Everything has an apple theme. From the apps to the cake.

"May we please introduce you to Mister and Missus Calvin McLane!" They announce us as *Perfect Duet*, by Ed Sheeran and Beyoncé begins.

I take her hand, and my heart swells as I listen to the words. I've never heard it before, but the song is *us*. Friends to lovers. Her belief in us. I pull her into me, trying to hide the tears that threaten to fall.

"What's the matter?" She lightly laughs, holding me.

"Oh!" I gasp. "I love you. So much. Nothing, no matter what, you *need* to know that."

"Silly rabbit. I know. *We know*." She pulls back and sees the tears. "You got me, and I got you, till the wheels fall off. Remember?" She tiptoes and brings me down to kiss her. *"Your's forever."*

The song ends, and we go over to our seats. They serve us, and we laugh, eat, and kiss the night away. I put on a happy face. Then I see *them*. Brynn, and Caryn. My eyes zero in, and my stomach lurches. Kaycee is talking to her mom by the soda bar. She doesn't see.

I covertly make my way over, they see me, and their smiles turn devilish. I grab them both by the arm. "What the fuck are you doing here?"

"Well- I was invited," Brynn smirks. "By you before we started fucking?"

"Would you shut up?"

"Why don't want people to know you're a coke whore, who'll suck clit for a bump?"

I cover her mouth and drag her outside

with Caryn on our heels.

"Why? What could you have to gain from being here? Either of you?'

"Oh, I'm just here to see the train wreck. You know father and mother are divorcing because of you?" Caryn lets out a loud burp. Her cigarette ash falling to the ground.

"Put that shit out."

"You really are a boring shit." She scoffs, flicking the thing at me. "When I heard you'd gotten a habit, I thought maybe we'd have some fun. Guess not."

"What do you want? *Money*? I—I got like three hundred bucks. Here get lost."

"I want your big cock, in me."

"I wanna watch."

"You?" I look at them both. "You're sick, both of you."

"Whatever. Good luck—oh, by the way, you've been transferred to the Spring Street shop. Think I wasn't gonna find out you put in for my job? Fucking traitor." Brynn spits in my face walking away.

"See ya round little bro." Caryn smirks following after what I see now is her friend. They laugh hard as Caryn grabs Brynn by the ass. I put a hand to my head. Was I set up? Was this all to ruin me and Kaycee? Was it all just a trap, and did it succeed?

"Hey?' I turn, feeling Kayce before I hear her.

"Was that your sister?"

I nod.

"What is she doing here?'

"Trying to goad me. I didn't let her."

"Good." She turns me to her. "I'm tired of

this dress. Take me to our room and help me out of it?" She smiles. "Please, Mister McLane."

"I like the sound of that."

CHAPTER 42

KAYCEE

"Calvin!" I'm screaming as they shove me into the ambulance. Just as I ask my husband to ravish me, my water brakes. In front of everyone! It seems what I thought was hunger pangs and gas all day was my early labor! The venue calls 911, and they are rushing me back to Philly, where my doctor will be waiting for us. "CALVIN ARCHER MCLANE!"

"I—I'm here!" He hops into the back of the ambulance. "I had to give my keys to Uncle Douglas. They're gonna meet us after they square up the party." He sniffs, wiping his face.

He's sweaty and looks freaked out as he grabs my hand. "Okay, let's try and remember you're breathing."

"Yeah? You try it, while you feel like somebody's trying to rip you in two!" I growl.

"Okay, Miss-"

"Missus!" Me and Cal correct the EMT.

"Sorry, Missus, McLane. We need to get these monitors on your belly, so we need to get this dress off you."

I whimper. "You're gonna cut it?"

"Well do you have-"

"Unbuckle me and unzip me. I don't care if you all see my underwear, but you ain't cutting up my dress-damnit!" I bark.

The EMTs look to Cal who chuckles. "I wouldn't argue with her."

They get me out of my dress, and they're eyes pop and lips purse. I've got on a lacy strapless pushup, full garters with white fishnets and lace boy short panties. "Hey, It was my wedding night. What do you expect?"

"I love it." Cal pushes the EMT out of the way and kisses me, just as a contraction starts. I punch him in the gut. "Ugh!' He falls back.

"Sorry, my husband. It's *painful*." I groan. They cover me with sticky things and a blanket as we zip down the highway toward the hospital.

When we arrive, they take me to the maternity ward while Cal finishes up the paperwork and gets set up to join me.

"It's going to be fine, Kaycee, you're doing great." The EMT who's name is Greg assures me. "Your husband ran to the bathroom; he'll be right in."

"Th-thank you." I grit out through another contraction. They're fifteen minutes apart.

"Hello, seems we're looking to have a baby, aren't' we?" Doctor Benedetti smiles, coming in almost getting knocked down by Cal.

"S-sorry." He stutters.

What the hell is up with him? Is he drunk?

"It's fine. Let's just see where we're at, huh?"

The doc gets me up in the stirrups and pops the hood. "Okay, you're at five centimeters; we still have a ways to go."

"There's more?" I whine.

"Yes, dear. Afraid so."

"Drugs! I want pain killers, *now*."

"Soon, okay? We need to be able to accurately keep track of things, and an epi too soon can slow the process. We need to wait a bit more."

"Oh, I'm never doing this again!"

The doc snickers. "We all say that, then we wind up right back here." She looks to Cal. "Are you alright? You look a bit peaked."

"Just nervous for her. Hot too, I gotta change out of this wool suit ya know?" He smiles.

"*Okay...* Well, if you need anything. I'll be back in a bit to see where we're at."

I reach out. "You're leaving?"

"Just going out to the nurse's station to get some paperwork in order. I'm not going far. You are not being abandoned, besides you got people who want to see you."

I let out a moan, as mom and grandpa come in. Cal kisses me and disappears with his bag to the bathroom.

"Hey, baby." Mom says, rubbing my lower back.

"That feels good.." I say, my eyes rolling. "Don't *stop*." Another contraction, has me crying out, and Cal stumbling out from the bathroom, pulling up his sweatpants.

"Kayce, you okay?"

"No! You did this to me!"

"Me! You let me! For my birthday!" He squawks back.

"Oh sure, tell *everyone*!"

"I just won't be blamed in total for something we both wanted to do, *repeatedly*!"

"You're such a jerk!"

"You're adorable when you're mad!" He laughs.

"You two, seriously!" Grandpa shakes his head. Looking Cal over. "Are you alright, son?"

"Why do you all keep asking that?" He sniffs. Wiping his face. "I'm fine."

"Cal, is something wrong?" I ask, seeing him fidget and twitch.

"Oh, my God! Can't I just be anxious?" He holds his arms around himself, and Grandpa grabs him. Staring him in the face.

"What are you on?"

Cal recoils. "N-It's-Nothing!"

"I need a nurse!" Grandpa calls out, keeping Cal from leaving the room. "Sit, you-stupid boy."

Cal sits as the nurse comes in. "I need you to do vitals-I think he's high."

"Sir I-"

"Just a general assessment, *please*, my granddaughter is about to have this idiot's baby."

The nurse nods gently and takes stock of my husband as I watch helplessly, unable to stop them.

"Well, his pupils are severely dilated, heartbeat is well over the normal rate, and his aggressiveness all suggests some sort of substance and the bit of white in the back of the throat suggests at least to me, cocaine or another powdered substance. But I'm not a doctor."

"It's nothing, I-I'm fine." Cal protests. "This is bull shit. You all-you just want me out of here, don't you? Just like my family." Cal looks at me, desperate. "Kayce, I-I'm fine; I swear it's nothing."

"Nothing? Like that woman you were talking to at the reception that was telling people she knew you intimately?" Grandpa asks. "I thought she was just drunk. Now I'm wondering."

"Brynn? She's a slut-It was nothing."

He isn't denying it. My chest is starting to tighten, and *my* heart rate is going up. The monitors are starting to scream, and so am I. "Get out!" I grit my teeth.

"Kayce?" Cal tries to touch me, and I punch him square in the face. "Get the fuck out of here! Get out of our house! I don't want to see you!" I sob as the nurses come into see to me. The orderlies come as I keep screaming for them to take him out. My contractions come, and I'm blinded by unimaginable pain.

CHAPTER 43

CALVIN

My son is born. At nine-fifteen September fifteenth two thousand and nineteen. Weighing seven pounds six ounces and just under nineteen inches long. Where was I? Not there where I should have been. Nope, instead, I was in the parking lot of the hospital, stoned out of my mind. I finished the baggie I had gotten from Walter before leaving the reception to go to the hospital. I thought, what was the hurt in taking the edge off? I guess I took off *too* much edge.

She threw me out. Not just of the room but of the house. She said to get out of *our* house. I'm hoping she will realize she was just angry and in pain from the labor. That we will be okay now that it's over. Grandpa sent me a picture of them asleep. They're beautiful. I'll go to them in the morning. After I clean up and change. He'll need his Hobbes anyhow. We don't have the baby bags or her stuff; it's all at the house. Right now, I just need to get home and sleep...

***

"Hey! Wake up. You can't be here." I wake to hear Tracie's voice as I'm kicked in the shin. I hit the couch and didn't get any farther.

"Says who? I live here?" I shield my eyes from the sun.

"She told you she wanted you out."

"Yeah? Figured she'd change her mind, I want to talk to her."

"Not a good idea. The only reason I haven't fucked you up is that I owe you, for saving her once. So you get one pass."

I sit up. "I fucked up, Tracie. I need to be able to fix it."

"What you've done, I couldn't forgive. You showed up to the birth of your child high! HIGH CALVIN! Who does that?" She smacks me. "How could you! You've not only broken her heart but mine and Compton's too! We love you! I went to bat for you! You little shit, and you fuck it all up! Get out! Get your shit and go somewhere. Get your shit together, or don't that's up to you. If you think for a second that you are getting anywhere near Kaycee or that innocent little baby like you are now, you are sorely mistaken." Grabbing me, she yanks me off the couch and tosses me to the floor. I take it. I deserve it.

I'm in tears, but I don't respond. I pull myself up and just go get my things. A duffle of clothes, my school stuff, and my credit cards. She watches me sternly. Tears in her bloodshot eyes.

"Please make sure she gets the keys to the Santa Fe; she's gonna need it."

"She'll manage."

"Don't punish her because I fucked up."
"Fine, thank you."

I nod, grabbing my bike and giving Stetson a pat I'm out the door.

***

A week. Then two. By week three, I'm losing my mind. I've never gone this long without talking to Kaycee. Not even when we were thirteen, and she had her tonsils out. We wrote letters and passed them back and forth through the fort in the woods between our houses. I'd play after school, and she'd play during the day since she couldn't go to school. I'd find notes about her day, and I'd tell her about mine. This was agonizing.

Staying high is my option; it lets me numb the sensations of loss. Brynn is still willing to supply me; I just have to let her suck my cock or whatever. If Kaycee doesn't want me anymore, what does it matter? I don't much care. I'm not going to class anymore. Don't care about that either. Nothing matters. All that glitters isn't gold, and all I ever wanted is fucking dust in the wind. So I'll ride the white lightning and tune it out. Maybe I'll find oblivion at the end of a straw.

CHAPTER 44

KAYCEE

"Calvin is a month old today. It also marks a month since I've seen or heard from his father. I thought he would have shown up to grovel or apologize. Thought he would have just been here when I came home. Instead, I came back to his side of the room emptied. Like some roommate that just skipped out on the rent. No note. *Nothing*. I guess that is my fault. I told him to go." I sigh, looking at the faces around me. My SARC group here in Philly isn't like the one from Cradle Bay. These people don't *know* Cal. To them, he's just another loser ex. Just another *junkie*.

"Grandpa is staying with me right now, so I'm not all alone. I wish he would just go. His *we McLane's stick together. We roll, we adapt*, shit is really getting old. I just want to sleep, but I know I have to take care of Calvin. If it wasn't for him... Well, I'm not really sure what I would do."

"Have you thought about hurting yourself, Kaycee?" Melina, the counselor, asks me, leaning forward somewhat.

"*What*? No, I mean. I just- I'm really sad.

I've lost my best friend in the whole world. Here I am with this wonderful, little boy, who's doing these amazing things, and all I want to do is share them with Cal. Cal's not there, yet every time I look at this baby, it's like looking at him, and it rips my heart out all over again. You know Calvin giggled yesterday, his first real one. I was pumping, and the suction thing slipped, and I tripped up, so my body went one way, and the rest of me another. That got him going real good. All I thought was *Cal; you gotta come here..."* I wipe a tear from my cheek. "I just miss him. Ya know?"

"You can't keep doing this. He chose. The drug over family. Nothing to be done." Cee-Cee, one of the women in the group, speaks up. "I'm sorry you got it rough, but at least your shits being handled. You got a support system. You don't need his shady ass."

Melina clasps her hands together with her telltale sign the group is about over, as Vicki comes out, looking around. She spies me and smiles. Walking over, she leans down. "He's awake; I think he's hungry."

I nod, getting up. "Excuse me. the feeder is needed." I chuckle picking up my bag and following Vicki to the playroom where they have been kind enough to keep an eye on Calvin while I participate in my group.

"There's my little chub." I smile and coo. He beams up at me, fussing a bit. I lift him, he's dry, so I'm sure it's the food he wants. I've been unable to get him to latch properly, so I'm pumping and bagging my milk to bottle for him. I have a portable warmer I bring with me everywhere. Plugs into the wall or the car and saves me a lot of time and trouble. I get Calvin situated and rock him gently as the bottle warms up.

"He's a good boy." Vicki smiles. "So quiet."

"For you, at home, he's restless and cranky most days."

"Maybe he feels your anxiety?"

"Maybe." The timer dings, and I get him fed. After changing him, I load him into the carrier, and we head back toward home. I'm sitting at a light when I notice a bit of red glint out the corner of my eye. Turning my attention, I see the neon of a pawn shop. Outside is a metallic grey Beaumont seven-speed with a green racing stripe. I double-take it. Then a honk pulls me out of my studious action. I have to go through the light. I make a mental note of the location of the shop.

"Grandpa?" I holler getting in the house.

"Yeah, Seabee?" He hollers back.

"Listen, can you watch Calvin?" I hand the baby off. "There are bottles in the fridge, and you know where all his other stuff is. I— I gotta go see about something."

"Is everything okay?"

"I really don't know. I'll be back as soon as I can." I stutter through as I kiss Calvin and rush back out the door

Getting back to the pawnshop, I see the bike is still there. It wasn't my imagination; it wasn't a mirage. I head inside.

Behind the screen sits a pudgy little man, playing a game of solitaire and smoking a cigar. "Um, excuse me?"

"What can I do ya for toots?"

"The Beaumont with the green stripe out front?"

"You talkin 'bout the bike?"

"Yeah, where'd you get it?"

He looks up at me. Sizing me up. He must smell the desperation on me. "What's it worth to you?"

"I just asked a simple question."

"No, you're asking me to pull records and look up a name, *possibly* an address." He licks his lips. "So, what's it worth?"

"How about I flash you and let you take a pic?" I say with a deep sigh.

He sneers, as he leers at me salaciously. "A'ight. Beaver too."

"Tits only, and I'm lactating, so you get a real show."

"Done."

I lift my top, and he snaps his pictures. "I'll give you five hundred to suck you off."

"Pass," I say, dropping my top back to my waist. "Now, about the bike."

"Yeah, let me look." He shuffles away and comes back. "ID says Calvin McLane, address,-"

"I know the address, but was they guy— I fish into my wallet and pull out our engagement photo. "Did he look like this?"

He snorts. "Yeah, maybe when you *knew* him. That guy's gone, guy, I got—looked a few meals shorter and a whole lot *higher*."

"You wouldn't know where he is?"

"Last I saw him; he was panhandling, among other things, down Southside."

"Southside?" I repeat. "Thank you."
He looks at his phone. "Thank *you*."

***

It takes me about an hour of searching before I decide that I'm going to have to have to venture out on foot. Parking, I wrap my coat around me, and with my photo in my hand, I start to show it to people. No one, of course, has seen Cal. It starts to get dark. Cooler and the vagrants start to migrate toward the underpasses. I too head that way, hoping a bit of money and food might bring them around. I bought pizzas, fifteen of them and two cases of Miller Lite.

Each person that comes up to get something I show the picture to, heads shake no. Then one lady pulls me aside.

"That's *Calvin*."

"Y-Yes," I say tears in my eyes.

"You're Kaycee? The one he talks about."

I nod.

"She left him here. Tossed him out of the car, shivering and broken."

"Who? Where is he?"

"He had been here but got sick. Took him to UPenn Hospital a few days ago. He's probably still there."

"Thank you." I hug her and sprint for the Santa Fe.

CHAPTER 45

CALVIN

I linger. In and out of consciousness. I don't really know where I am. I know it's warm, and the bed is softer than the mattress I had been sleeping on. The light hurts my eyes. My mouth is dry; I hurt all over. I just need to sleep.

I dream about Kaycee. Imagine she's here. Hear her voice. Hear Grandpa Compton and a baby too. That's not right. They left me. Or made me leave them. Either way, they're gone, and I'm alone. This pain wracks me, and I need to get up. I try but find I'm strapped in.

"Let me up!" I scream only to be helped down. *Sedated?* Ahh, sweet oblivion. I'm in a hospital. *Good drugs.*

Feeling a cool cloth on my head, I open my eyes to a dim room and beautiful bird blue eyes. I swallow, feeling the tears well up in my dry eyes. "Kayce?" I manage to croak. She's got her hair tied up in an all-over bun. She looks tired, stressed. Her hand glides over my forehead with the cool rag.

"I'm here." She whispers. "Do you know

where you are?"

"Hospital?" I try getting up, but I'm still strapped down. "Why?"

"You've been withdrawing, got violent. They had to strap you down for everyone's safety." She looks down at my hand as it fishes for hers, she steps back slightly. "I'll get the doctors."

"Kayce?" I call after her, but I have no volume. As she walks briskly away, I feel a dark shadow descend on me.

"You finally hit bottom, kid." Grandpa Compton says next to my ear. "The only way left to go is up."

I nod. "I'm so-sorry."

His hand clasps my shoulder. "It's alright, boy. You're gonna get help. If you want it."

"I want *her*."

"It can't be promised."

"I know."

"She's still in love with you, hasn't left your side in two weeks."

"Two?"

The doctor comes in, and the orderlies are with him. "Good evening, Mister McLane. It's nice to see you awake, and coherent. It's been a struggle, but here you are."

"Can we maybe get these off me?"

"Oh, sure, sure. Just a moment."

The orderlies remove my restraints, and I am assisted to sit up. They explain to me that I presented as an overdose, with multiple fractures to my right hand, a radial fracture to my right arm, and a dislocated collarbone.

***

"I vaguely remember what happened. It was humiliating. Having to explain to the doctors and the police officers, that I was using. That the people, Walter Bradley and Brynn Kohl, my ex-manager at Verizon who were my suppliers, beat me up and robbed me. I had to own up to the panhandling, the sex trading, all of it. I had to watch as the love of my life took in what I'd done. Watch the disgust, and disappointment cross her face. I lost her in those moments." I trail off seeing the tears in the faces of the other Narcotics Anonymous members. "Anyhow, I got out of the hospital and into a meeting. Today makes six months. Six months clean and serene as they say." They clap, I lower my head humbled. "I couldn't do it if I didn't fall. I had to scrape the bottom, but Grandpa Compton was right, there's only one way to go from there, and that's up. Every day I take a step. You can too. It works, keep coming back. Thank you."

I pocket my little plastic chip and sit back down. It's almost three-thirty. Almost time for my supervised visit with Calvin. It took a lot of work, but Kaycee has finally agreed to allow me to see him. I've missed so much. Lost the trust I took years to gain. My own fault, of course, but I'm prepared to put in the work to get it back.

CHAPTER 46

KAYCEE

The doorbell rings. I'm a nervous wreck. Cal hasn't been in the house with me since the night before our wedding. We're still married. *Technically*. Mom said I should have filed for an annulment, but I can't. I just-can't. He's the father of my child, the only man I ever wanted to call husband. I promised him forever. Right now, it's just; we're in need of a little tune-up. We said until the wheels fell off, well we sorta forgot to put the chains on them, hit the black ice, and landed in a ditch. Of course, my mother's meddling didn't help. It hurt to know that she sent him away, that she was the reason he was gone so long without a word. I was angry, but still, it had to be done.

I open the door and there he stands. Just a little over a year, since we were first together in my mom's house, in our little fort. The safe place he made for us, the night the first promises were made. He looks good, healthy. Hair clipped short, face cleanly shaven. It makes him look older somehow. He smiles, meekly at me. "Hi."

"Hey." I open the door. "You wanna come in?"

He nods, and I can't help but watch his ass in those fitted jeans as he walks by me. I feel the old familiar feelings creep up my spine. Pushing it down, I close the door.

"Everything's the same." He looks around.

"No reason to change it." I pick up a couple of toys from the floor. "Calvin's in the nursery. He's still napping, did you want a cup of coffee?"

"Decafe?"

"Um- no. I may have- I got herbal tea? That's decaffeinated."

"Okay." He nods, following me into the kitchen.

"When did you stop drinking coffee?" I ask, taking down the teapot and blowing the dust off it with a chuckle. "It may need a rinse."

"No stimulants of any kind, not anymore. No caffeine, very little processed sugars, hell I hardly even eat chocolate, now."

"I'd die."

"I almost did." He answers quietly and looks at the floor.

"I'm sorry-"

"Don't you apologize to me, not ever. You didn't do anything. You didn't offer me the drugs or take them for me. I did that. I chose my path. I thought I could control it. Control my surroundings. In the end, all I managed to do was destroy the one thing that mattered to me. I know we'll never be the same."

"There's no going back. That's very true,

Cal. Though, maybe, there's a way to go forward? Let's see how these visits go. Okay?"

He nods, as the whistle on the pot blows I hear Calvin coo through the monitor. Cal is at the dining room table with Stetson, Abby and Titan are at his feet. Cletus and Kerry, my two newest additions to the family, watch him; they are a pair of Newfoundland mixes. Huge and shy, they take time to warm up to people, but they love the little chub.

"Can I go get him?" He asks me, and I nod. The dogs follow him, glued to him. Guess they miss him too.

I listen through the monitor as Cal engages his son.

"Hey there. I'm your daddy."

"Ma-ma-" Calvin is starting to talk but only just. I hear him fuss, then settle. I'm guessing Cal picked him up.

"You need a diaper, huh? Okay. Well, let's see where that is."

This should be amusing. I head upstairs to observe.

Cal is with us for about two hours. Any more and I may have not let him leave. He's good with Calvin. Sweet, sitting on the floor with him. Engaging him, talking to him, not at him. Somebody's read a few books. He kisses Calvin goodbye, and we have an awkward exchange, I have Calvin in my arms to keep his daddy at length. As soon as he's out the door, I shut and lock it before bursting into tears.

***

"He's just been so good with him," I say to Micha. We've been in touch a lot since the split, and he's been my rock. My safe place. Someone I could talk to who wouldn't judge me. He may be a kid, but he's wise beyond his years.

"You still love him?"

"With all of me and more."

"Does he know that?"

"I haven't *not* told him."

"Sheesh woman, you can't fix it if you don't talk about it."

"I just don't know that I can trust in him again. He's back in school, working, volunteering. How would he cope with us too? It was having too much that put him in the spot to do the drugs. I don't want to tip his scale again."

"Girl, you need to take the leap, or you need to let him go. It's your choice, but it's not fair to either of you to keep yourselves penned up in this state of limbo."

"I know... *I know.*" I wipe my hand down my face, looking at the clock. He'll be here for his weekly visit soon. "Listen, I gotta go."

"Give him my love and yours." Micha sighs, hanging up.

CHAPTER 47

CALVIN

Eight weeks. Eight visits with my son. Some with Kaycee, some with Compton. All mostly filled with uncomfortable silences. Compton made it very clear that he wants to be able to trust me, but it's just too soon for him, and Kaycee? She can barely stay in the same room with me for very long. She observes, but from a distance.

I have some happy moments, I may have missed a lot of firsts, but I was here today when Calvin finally stood up and walked. He's learning who I am, calling me da-da. He hugs me and kisses me now. I'm starting to actually feel like a *dad*. A *real* one. I look up from playing with the ball on the floor. Stetson was in on it, so it's been fun. I see Kaycee watching us with a smile. When she realizes I've spotted her, she drops her eyes and goes back to fussing in the kitchen. The smells coming from there are making my stomach growl. At some point, she seems to have learned to cook.

I get up, putting Calvin in his pen before approaching her. "What have you got cooking?"

"Making a mint jelly. For the lamb, I'm making for tomorrow."

I look at her, confused.

"Easter Sunday?"

"Is it? I hadn't realized."

"So, you don't have anywhere to be?" Kaycee watches me closely.

"No, guess I'll get a TV dinner and watch King of Kings."

"You could bring the movie here; I have a Blue-ray player now." She points at the tv. "It's just going to be us. Mom and Douglas are in New York, and Grandpa is seeing a nice woman from the lodge, so he's having dinner with her."

"So, you're making a lamb for just you?"

"I picked up a small rack, figured I'd have leftovers, but if you'd rather not-"

"No-no, I'd love to. What can I bring? Besides the movie? *Anything?*"

"Some snacks, a basket for Calvin, maybe?"

"I can do that." I look around; it's about time I left. "Okay, well, Calvin's in his pen, so I'm gonna head home. What time tomorrow?"

"Three?"

"Three is it."

I leave Kaycee and head straight for a meeting. The idea of seeing her again tomorrow for more than just a couple of hours stresses me. When I'm stressed, I want to use.

"Cal, you're a good man, you're here, and not down Southie." Rikki, my sponsor, assures me.

"I know, I just-my hopes are up. She's invited me to dinner *and* a movie."

"Sounds banal enough."

"You don't know, *Kaycee*. The last time we did dinner and a movie, I wound up tangled in twinkle lights."

"*That* sounds like a good time, but I can see your concern. Look take it for face value. You are alone on a family holiday. She sees that and thinks you deserve to be with your little boy. Don't read any more into it."

"Right. One step at a time, one day at a time."

"Exactly. *Stay* calm, *stay* focused. You'll be fine."

"Thanks, Rikki."

"Anytime."

***

Sunday comes, and I've dressed nicely, button-down, slacks, my hair combed neatly, even with the helmet. Yeah, I got my bike back. Took a bit of time, but I never lost my ticket, and no one wanted the damn thing anyway. I got a small basket with chocolates and a little white bunny for Calvin and another with a little pink bear for Kaycee. Loaded her's with Cadbury cream and caramel eggs. She loves those. I brought her favorite snacks, too, plus the popcorn with *extra* butter.

I knock and hear her fussing by the door with the dogs. She opens the door, and my breath hitches.

She's in pink, from her peep-toe heels to her dangle earrings. The dress she's wearing is cut to the knee and spaghetti-strapped. Fitter at the waist but full at the hip. Kaycee has her hair pulled up and back from her face, and her makeup is on point, pretty and blush pink.

"Wow." I can't keep it to myself.

"Thanks, come in?"

I hand her the daylilies I picked up on my way over. She smiles from ear to ear, and she's just made my year.

I watch her as she goes and sets them on the table that's set for us.

"There are apps over in the living room. Deviled eggs, pigs in blankets, cheeses, and meats with crackers. I got flavored waters, with and without fizz, or milk, juices?"

"I'll take fizzy water any flavor." I head for the playpen and my boy.

Calvin is up and already calling Da-da. I pick him up, kissing him. "Hey, Calvin, how are you?" I smile as she comes over with the water. "Can I help at all?"

"I'm about to put the bread in; then we can eat. Did you want to feed him?"

"Could I?"

"Sure." She points to his high chair. "Just get him there, and I'll get his food. Then we can have relative peace for a while.

"Sounds good." I watch her; she's still a knockout. In fact, I think she's hotter now than she was *before* we got married. God, how I miss her. I just wish I could tell her.

CHAPTER 48

KAYCEE

"Thank you." Cal says while we have a quiet dinner.

"You're welcome, but I'm not sure what you're thanking me for."

"For this? For letting me see Calvin, for never serving me."

I'm quiet. I'm not sure how to respond at first. "Well, I couldn't very well have you sitting in that stuffy little apartment of yours eating a tv dinner when I was having such a good meal, not today. As for letting you see Calvin. Of course, so long as you stay clean and sober, I have no issue with you being in his life. In *our* lives. Now when it comes to not serving you with divorce papers..." I sigh. "Cal, I'll be honest. I have them. I've looked them over; mom wanted me to fill them out months ago. I just *couldn't*."

"Why not? I mean, I fucked you over pretty good."

I nod. "Yeah. You did. Yet here you are, eight months later, sitting across from me, bent, but not broken. I nearly lost you, and that scared the shit out of me. I made you a promise, of forever. I meant it."

"So did I. When we were dancing, I told you, I love you, that you needed to know that no matter what when I took my vows, I never meant to break them."

"But you did." I look down at my hands at my rings. I've never taken them off. He reaches across the table and takes my hands.

"Kaycee, the way I feel has never wavered. Not for an instant. The flesh is weak, but my heart was and has always been yours. Do with it what you will. I am your slave." He drops to his knees and puts his head in my lap. My instinct is to run my hands through his hair.

I start to and stop, sighing. "*Cal...*"

"*Please...* I need a second chance. I swear to you I will not waste it. I will spend the rest of my life, proving myself to you if I must. I'm crazy about you. I love *you*, love our *son*. I want to make other babies with you. I want to make that life with you."

My fingers play with his hair, and I nod- not that he can see. My tears are big and ugly. A large sob escapes my lips. "My silly rabbit." He looks up. "Kiss me, before I change my mind."

He's up on his knees-his hands on my hips. Crushing me against him, he kisses me, and I melt into him. In seconds he's pulling my panties to my ankles and opening my legs to indulge himself in my ripened peach. I let out a ravenous moan. I haven't been touched since before Calvin came, and Cal knows just what I need. His tongue flicks and teases my clit. What's this? His tongue? It's-

"Christ You got your tongue pierced?"

"All for you." He smirks coming up just to answer before diving back down to make me squirm once more. The dogs start to get upset, so he gets up, and puts them all outside. This gives me time to think.

"Cal, we can't do this. I don't' think-"

He lifts me up and holding me, so we're belly to belly he kisses me once more. "Please, let me make you come."

"I- *Okay.*" I answer finally as he carries me up to our bed. Stripping me, he licks and kisses every inch of my flesh as it exposes. Fingers, to toes. He makes me moan, whimper, and call his name, all with just his mouth! Then he gets his hands involved. He unravels me like a kitten with a ball of yarn.

It takes hours before we even begin to make love, and by the time we do, I'm so wet he just slips inside and fills me up like he hasn't been gone more than half a year. We have to stop to care for Calvin, but then he pulls me back to bed and ravages me again.

***

Morning comes, and I find I'm alone, but there is a text on my phone.

Calvin: Kayce, I love you more than you will ever know. I had to go home to get ready for class. But would love to see you later? Call me at noon. Talk to you soon.

I bite my lip, I feel wonderful, even if I

shouldn't have done what I did. You know what? I don't care what anyone thinks, he's my husband damnit, and if I want to fuck my estranged husband on a whim on Easter Sunday, I damn well will. I'll tell you another thing, if he comes over again today, I'm gonna let him indulge again and again because I've been neglected for way too long and need to let go of all this pent up energy.

CHAPTER 49

CALVIN

Certified Peer Specialist Training. That is what my Mondays consist of nowadays. I found the department of behavioral health site as a fluke looking for work that would get me out of the retail environment and into the counseling one as I've changed my major from Law to Psych. I need to understand my addiction. I figure the better I understand the disease, the better equipped I am to fight the fucker.

The CPS is a person who has life experience with mental and or behavioral situations that can be considered relatable to those in recovery. In other words, other addicts, in recovery. People like me. There's a bit of paperwork and training, but in the end, you get paid to work your program and help others to work theirs. You tell your story, your *truth*, in the hopes it *helps* others.

Today's truth was that I was just in bed with my wife and baby momma but have no idea what that even means. Was it a one-time thing? Are we getting back together? Was it just an itch that needed scratching? One step forward, two steps back. I feel like a broken record, but I'll manage, even if it's short-lived today ain't nothin' gonna break my stride.

Noon comes, and I'm done for the day. As if on cue, my phone rings.

"Yeah?"

"Hey."

"Hey, you called." I smile though she can't hear that.

"You asked me to."

"I was-wasn't sure, though."

"I-no-are ya busy?"

"Just finished up a class, was gonna get lunch, you and Calvin fancy a stroll up *Woodland walk*, maybe lunch at *KQ Burger*?

"Hmm, sounds delicious, give us fifteen?"

"Yeah, I'll hold a table for us."

"Just order me the mushroom burger with crispy onions and bacon, oh plus cheese fries and a Sprite."

"Gotcha."

***

Kaycee shows in ten. I'm just sitting with the food, and she's got Calvin in her arms. Sitting him in a high chair, she smiles, kissing me on the cheek hello. *Progress*!

"Oh, I'm starving." She sits stuffing a fry in her mouth, which has Calvin fussing. "I've got your share, don't you worry." She looks at me, and her eyes sparkle. "Boy want's everything I eat these days."

"Well, you do eat the good stuff. I wouldn't want that mush if I could have a burger."

"Right?" She looks back at me with a chuckle as she situates him.

"So-about last night."

"Could we not make a thing about that?" She cuts me off. Then stops, sighing. "I'm not regretting it, by all means, I had-I mean being with you has always been-" She blushes. "You know what you can do. It's just that I'm not entirely ready for you to just come home. Not *yet*."

"No, I understand. It's too soon." My heart sinks.

"Cal, please. I want to keep seeing you. I want you to keep seeing us. I've been thinking about it, all morning. Everyone else is going on with their lives. Mom and Douglas with the baby. Grandpa and his girlfriend. It's time we all moved forward too. So how about this? I let you see Calvin *more*?"

"How much is more?"

"Three nights a week? So I can go back to work. Bills need to be paid, and the work from home gigs are drying up."

"I could do that. My place-or?"

"Oh, no-definitely our home. I mean, all his stuff is there."

I nod. "Right. Makes sense, and *us*?"

"We play it by ear. Try dating. Worse case, end up friends again."

"Kayce, were *married*."

"Yes, I know. I don't see that changing either. I love you, that's not going to change either." She reaches across the table, taking my hand. "This is the best I can offer you right now. It's not happily ever after. It's more like we'll see how it goes."

"I'll take it."

We finish our lunch and packing Calvin into the jogger stroller take him to the park. It's a beautiful day, and with any luck, it won't be our last.

~To New Beginnings~

Special Information
This book has touched on a few difficult subjects. Know that there is help out there. The agencies mentioned are *real* and can aid. You are not alone.

Support, Advocacy & Resource Center (SARC)
http://supportadvocacyresourcecenter.org/about-sarc.html

Supplemental Nutrition Assistance Program (SNAP)
https://www.fns.usda.gov/snap/supplemental-nutrition-assistance-program-snap

Women, Infants, and Children (WIC)
https://www.fns.usda.gov/wic/women-infants-and-children-wic

Planned Parenthood
https://www.plannedparenthood.org/

Narcotics Anonymous (NA)
https://www.na.org/

SPECIAL INFORMATION

This book has touched on a few difficult subjects know that there is help out there. The agencies mentioned are *real* and can aid. You are not alone.

Support, Advocacy & Resource Center
(SARC)
http://supportadvocacyresourcecenter.org/about-sarc.html

Supplemental Nutrition Assistance Program
(SNAP)
https://www.fns.usda.gov/snap/supplemental-nutrition-assistance-program-snap

Women, Infants, and Children
(WIC)
https://www.fns.usda.gov/wic/women-infants-and-children-wic

Planned Parenthood
https://www.plannedparenthood.org/

Narcotics Anonymous
(NA)
https://www.na.org/

PENNED STATE

About S.I. Hayes

S.I. Hayes was born and bred in New England, currently living in Ohio. Running around Connecticut, she used all of her family and friends as inspiration for her many novels. When not writing any multitude of genres, she can be found drawing one of many fabulous book covers or teasers. To see them, check out [Haney Hayes Promotions](www.haneyhayespr.com). www.haneyhayespr.com

In 2016 she partnered with J. Haney, and they are now colloquially known as The Deviant Darlings, who have been on the journey of a thousand tales. Their joy for writing and helping authors led to the launch of Haney Hayes Promotions (HHP), an Author Services Company that helps authors from the ground up. Be they just starting out or have accolades like USA Today or Wallstreet Journal, HHP strives to give every author they work with the support they need so that they can do what they love.

Keep your eyes open and a fresh pair of panties close by. You know, just in case.

To find out more, join ARC teams, or become an Influencer, join the Deviant Darlings' mailing list. https://linktr.ee/s.i.hayes

mailing list
https://dashboard.mailerlite.com/forms/23226/68366423768958534/share

Also, by J. Haney & S.I. Hayes

(A County Fair Romance)
Wild Ride
Stolen Moments
Winter Kisses
Spring Fling
Freedom Rings
Hard Harvest
(A Sex, Drugs, and Rock Romance)
Vegas Lights
Hell in Heels
Tatted Up & Tied Down
(Working Class Beauties)
Avery
Mady
(The Adventures of Ana & Xav)
Catching Creole
(Temptations and Troubles in Downers Grove)
The Newbie
(Navy SEAL Liaisons)
Call Sign: Baby Daddy
(The Averdeen Duet)
Tell Me Tru
(A Blue Moon Riders Tale)
Alpha Encounters: Nomity
(What If...)
Stupid Cupid
(Royals of Aeterna)
Ascension
(Welcome To...)
Hollyhock: Yuletide
(Cherry Tree Heights)
Resolution
(Grey Gulls Landing)

Tangled Up in Blue
(Devil Dogs)
Unbroken
(Bishop Cliffs)
Shafted
(Runaway)
Landing the Runaway
(Shadow Academy)
Incandescence

(Stand Alone Novels)
Under His Skin
Love at Rincon Point
MisGiving Hearts
Rising Star
Irish Eyes And Mafia Lies
Sweet Intentions
Island Heir
Un-Leashed
Faking It
12 Days of Christmas
Music Heals the Heart
Call Him Baker
Sitting Pretty

Also, by S.I. Hayes

(The Wrath Saga)
Awakenings
(The Roads Trilogy)
In Dreams… The Solitary Road
In Dreams… The Unavoidable Road
In Dreams… The Savage Road
(Centuries of Blood)
Becoming

(The Natural Alpha)
California Moon
(Guardians of Grigori)
Fated Binds
Midnight Run
Branded Wings
Faery Road
(Manhattanites)
Xander & Asher
(A PARKS Sector Selection)
Chasing Shadows
(Young Hearts)
Penned State

(Stand Alone Novels)
Administrative Duties
Heart of Stone
Battleborn
Sweet Girls
Friends & Lovers

Made in United States
Orlando, FL
29 April 2024